I0738573

Other books by Annie Russell:

The Changeling : A New Orleans Faerie Tale
(The Faerie Tale Chronicles – Book One)

Of Ghosties and Ghoulies: A Handbook Of
Things That Go Bump In The Night.

Acknowledgments

No author works alone and I'm certainly no exception. There are so many people who were instrumental in helping this book come to fruition and I'd like you all to know how these incredible humans have come to my aid over the last year:

Dawn, my summertime beach-buddy and year-round friend, for introducing me to the legend of The Journey Stone on one of our many walks along the shores of Lake Michigan.

My editor, **Emory Elgar**, for her eagle-eye, love of language, and all-round good humor. I can't thank her enough for coming along on this journey with me through the land of Faerie Tales.

Jack Russell, Jr. for his invaluable skill at formatting text and his artistic and intuitive design creations for the cover art of the books.

I thank **Lisa S.** for her never-faltering support and **Jenniffer S.** for listening to plot strategies over and over again.

For **Mary A.** who graciously allowed me the literary use and visual images of her home.

Thank you to **Kim R., Kimberly H., and Kim G.** for reading bits and pieces and offering suggestions and guidance.

I am happily and forever indebted to my husband, **Jack**, for his steadfastness and strength. He reminded me throughout this writing that the impossible is almost always possible with dedication and laughter as a guide.

Inspiration and Knowledge always comes with a price; a lesson from The Fae that I hold dear.

For Annette -

May your Journeys throughout The Realms be
filled with love, peace, and joy.

Your laugh echoes in my dreams and your
smile lights my heart still.

The Journey Stone

A Charlevoix Faerie Tale

First hardcover edition November 2021

Edited by Emory Elgar
Layout by Jack Russell Jr.

ISBN 978-0-578-76139-8 (Hardcover)
ISBN 978-0-578-76140-4 (Paperback)

NoMi Press
annierussell.net

Prologue

As the sun set over Lake Charlevoix, turning the sky cotton candy-colored pinks and purples, the Witch ran down the wooded path to a small spring that sat at the edge of the sloped yard. The cedars lining the path spread far beyond the spring, and black outlines of the trees reflected in the water as the day's light fell into the pool.

The Witch didn't look like a Witch—not how people would imagine witches from storybooks. Her body was not draped in black robes, at least not currently, and she did not wear a tall, pointed hat, as those were only worn at Halloween parties. She didn't have any warts, her skin wasn't any shade of green, and her nose was perfectly shaped. Yet, a Witch she was, through both natural ability and years of training. Her talent was a gift she was born with. Her skill, however, had been hard-won over decades of study and practice. Decades of trials and tribulations, accomplishments, and accolades were all experienced within the circle of those who shared like-minds and like-hearts. At one time, magic was practiced and performed in Perfect Love and Perfect Trust until the practice became knotted and its ideals entangled. The hearts and minds within the group diverged; sides were taken, and new allegiances formed. Power, not Love, became the focus of the one vying for control, and try as she might, the Witch could no longer hold the center. The circle was broken. Though her spirits told her it was futile, she had pleaded her case to the others in the group, but the results were disastrous.

Now, as she stumbled down the path, tripping and catching her toes on cedar roots and the large stones found this close to the bay, she could feel the air around her grow heavy and ominous. The wolf was getting closer. Dragging a ragged breath into her burning lungs, the Witch ran headlong into the clearing that held the ancient spring and spun around to face the path that brought her here. Planting both feet firmly in the loamy soil, she gathered her scattered energy back into herself then sent it careening outward at the dark wolf-shaped mass that slunk down the path in her direction. Her owl, born of her magic and will, took flight and shot forward, prepared to not only defend its mistress but attack if necessary.

But the Witch had chosen her defense poorly. By putting all of her substantial energy into her owl's attack on the wolf, she had left her physical body vulnerable. This had, of course, been the plan of her attacker all along. Stepping into the clearing, the Witch's aggressor raised her hands over her head, palms open and fingers splayed. Dark-red sparks danced above her as she chanted the words that would remove the Witch, the one who had brought the coven to fruition but failed to recognize its power. As the assailant felt the magic gather around her, she reached into her pocket for the stone. She held the egg-sized, banded stone in her left hand, and with her right hand outstretched, fingers pointed at the Witch, she finished the incantation that would rid her of the problem.

The Witch felt the atmosphere around her change, and she became aware of whispered chanting. She turned in time to see her coven-mate, stone in one hand and the doll at her feet. Cherry-red sparks like malignant fireflies lit the tableau. Before she could react, the magic hit her square in the chest, and pressure that she had never felt before bore down on her. She cried out in pain and fear.

She felt rather than heard the last of the spell—screamed in triumph now rather than whispered—and began a terrifying free-fall into nothingness that contained neither light nor sound. It was utterly devoid of everything except a tremendous sense of gravity that caused the feeling of falling from a great height. She did not know for how long she fell.

Before the nothingness consumed her, the Witch sent an arc of magic born of sadness, anger, and betrayal that shot forth from her in an explosion of blue. The magic zipped through the trees, back up the trail, and hit the small house with an explosion of light. Within the house, the coven's candles flared setting the curtains alight. The flames spread to the rugs, furniture, and finally the walls as the structure that housed those who had betrayed her burned to the ground.

The assailant called the wolf back and felt it settle within her breast. The fire that hungrily consumed the coven's home was an unforeseen event, and she spat on the doll at her feet in hatred.

"You can never just let things be, can you? Always with the last word, it never fails!" she screamed as she kicked the doll into the cedar woods. After cautiously approaching the burning house, she ran down the trail as the fire truck's sirens blasted their way down the rural highway from the neighboring town of Boyne City.

The Witch landed, still bound by nihility, with a thump. Her vision was now limited to the wooded scenery that was directly in front of the doll's eyes. Finally realizing what had happened and having no idea how to escape, she retreated into her own thoughts allowing the darkness of oblivion to flow over her like water.

The owl had witnessed the magical events take place at the spring. Unlike the assailant's wolf, the owl was not entirely crafted from the energy of the Witch and could exist outside of her if needed. The owl watched as the one who tried to destroy his mistress ran toward the burning covenstead and sent forth a screech of pain and anger that caused her and her new followers to cringe in fear. He spread his massive wings and took flight, soaring high over the burning house, noting that all the humans had made it out of the inferno. With that information in mind, the great bird of prey flew back to the clearing at the spring, snatched up the porcelain doll, and flew over the dark waters of the bay toward the larger lake beyond.

As the moon began its slow ascent, the owl cruised silent and unseen above the small town of Charlevoix. Banking right over the drawbridge, he coasted over the stately homes along Michigan Avenue until he, moving the doll into his beak, landed in a pine tree across from the last house on the street. There were, of course, no lights on and no one at home. The homeowner had a meeting earlier in the day at a modest house thirteen miles away.

The owl lifted off from the pine branch, graceful despite its enormous size, and flew over the house to the gardens behind it. In one swift motion, he deposited the doll onto the flagstones at the back door then coasted up to the balcony that overlooked the manicured grounds and the cliffs that dropped into Lake Michigan. As still as any statue, the owl sat and watched as the moon moved along its course and the sun began to take its place. At dawn, the woman who cleaned and cared for the home arrived and took the doll inside. Satisfied, the owl took flight, cruising out and over the waters of the Lake until he disappeared into the cloud bank that hovered above the horizon.

Inside, the housekeeper wiped the morning dew off the doll and looked it over carefully. It was a large doll, standing easily two and a half feet tall and dressed in an ornate Victorian gown and feathered hat. She had never seen it before but thought it would fit perfectly on the decorative table next to the piano in the music room. The table had held a cut crystal vase until she accidentally dropped and broke it yesterday. The housekeeper dearly hoped that the homeowner wouldn't notice the swap as she carefully set the large doll into place. She positioned it so that it was visible from the entry's double doors and left to continue her dusting of the main floor's rooms.

The Witch opened her eyes to see the elegant sweep of the grand staircase and the main foyer in front of her. Using the limited amount of peripheral vision the doll allowed her, she could just make out the baby grand piano to her right and the door leading to the living room to her left. She was home.

Chapter 1

The balconies were empty, the streets were deserted, and the music was silent as Ashlynne walked home from another dismal night in Jackson Square. She stayed at her post later than normal hoping to attract one or two stragglers on their way back to their hotel room who might be willing to sit for a tarot reading, but there was no one. As she pulled her tote behind her, feeling it bump up and down over the uneven flagstones, Ashlynne mentally ran through her dwindling finances. Her scheduled hours at the speakeasy were nonexistent due to the lack of tourists, and tarot readings fell victim to the same situation. Being a service worker in a tourist town like New Orleans meant working in a boom-and-bust environment at the best of times. Lately, there was no 'boom,' and things looked dire. With her small nest egg of cash, including the money gifted to her from Mimi, she figured she had enough to either pay her rent for the rest of the summer or pay her rent until—hopefully—July and eat. Not both. Heaving a sigh full of frustration and anxiety, Ashlynne continued deeper into the French Quarter toward home.

As she crossed North Rampart Street and entered the Treme, Ashlynne's mood slipped from concern and anxiety to full-on panic. The drums that echoed through time from Congo Square seemed to quicken their pace to match her heartbeat. Ashlynne stood still on the corner of Ursulines Avenue and closed her eyes; jumbled images of dark-skinned dancers flashed behind her eyelids. Bodies swayed and moved to the beat of the drums as they danced between their time and her own, arms raised in both praise and supplication as their feet pounded the earth in ecstasy and anger. The dances were potent outlets for the rages and passions of the enslaved and mistreated in the city. When the Americans—with their restrictive and fearful approaches—took over New Orleans from the French, the dances and markets ceased, though the vibrations continued to influence the Treme for centuries. Ashlynne took great comfort knowing these visions were only echoes and imprints; the dancers were no longer held here.

She opened her eyes and took a deep breath to steady herself.

"Keep it together, there is always a way," she said out loud, her voice bouncing along the deserted street.

Not feeling one bit calmer, she pulled the wheeled tote that held her tarot reading setup down the final block toward home and felt it jump and bounce over the cracked and bulging sidewalks in cadence with the drumbeats.

Inserting her key into the ancient lock embedded in the louvered door on her side of the Creole double cottage, Ashlynne stepped into her living room, dragging the unwieldy tote behind her. While it was her preferred setup for getting tarot supplies from her house to Jackson Square, its two-wheeled design left much to be desired when it came to stairs and the downtown's uneven pavements.

"Hey there, buddy, how was your night?" she asked the dancing terrier at her feet.

She had to admit, no matter how pessimistic she felt, Murphy's all-in doggy grin never failed to lift her spirits, even if just a little bit. Ashlynne shoved her tote into the corner next to the bricked-over fireplace, dropped onto the sofa, and kicked off her sandals. Murphy, favorite bone in his mouth, settled at her feet—the picture of contentment. Absent-mindedly petting the wiry little dog with her right foot, Ashlynne continued to mentally gnaw at her own bone. What to do about the lack of jobs and income? It was only the end of April, but the scarce opportunities and tourists weren't likely to pick up this summer. In fact, they could worsen due to the oppressive heat and humidity that the summer months would bring. Round and round her thoughts went, obsessively trying out one idea only to dismiss it for another and then another. Well after midnight, Ashlynne's eyes were blurry and her limbs heavy from the exhaustion that constant worry invited.

"We could give up our lease here and find a cheaper place further uptown with roommates, Murph. What do you think?" she asked the dog at her feet. "But I don't know if I want roommates," she answered herself. "What if they smoke, or drink too much, or don't like dogs?" Murphy, secure in the knowledge that his human would figure it out one way or the other, kept working on his bone.

"You're no help at all," she admonished as she stood up, stepping over the dog and walking into the next room. There, she pulled the bed's coverlet back and changed into a clean t-shirt to sleep in. Winding her long hair up into a messy top knot, she padded barefoot into the kitchen and set the coffee maker to begin brewing in the morning.

Ashlynne walked back through her small apartment and into the front room. Nudging Murphy toward the bedroom and stooping down to get his bone, she caught movement out of the corner of her eye. She stood up.

"Hello, Dear," said the older woman in the full-length mirror that was propped against the wall next to the sofa.

"Mimi," Ashlynne smiled in greeting. "What's up?"

"Not a thing, Dear. You seem to be out of

sorts, so I thought I would stop by and say hello."

"Hello," chuckled Ashlynne, repeating the greeting.

"What's bothering you, Dear?"

"It's nothing," muttered Ashlynne, looking down and rubbing the floral area rug with her big toe. "I'm just tired, I guess."

On the other side of the glass, the spirit named Mimi pulled a straight-backed wooden chair from the left of the mirror's edge, sat down, and pulled a pack of Chesterfield Kings from the pocket of her housecoat. Striking a match on the glass and lighting her cigarette, she settled in. After inhaling deeply and exhaling an impressive array of smoke rings, she fixed Ashlynne with a stern look.

"Ashlynne, I know very well that you are not feeling like yourself. I'm sure you are tired but there's more."

"I appreciate your concern, Mimi, but I'm really fine."

"Then why is your light so dim? Your light is normally the brightest thing on this side of the glass—it's a beacon! It's how I found you. But now? Now it's dim and dull. Please tell me what's bothering you. Maybe I can help."

"There's no work, Mimi. The speakeasy is closed for now, and there are so few tourists in the Square that I haven't made more than fifty dollars a night in weeks. I'm scared," Ashlynne finished in a whisper.

Mimi continued to inhale the smoke and exhale rings while Ashlynne rubbed the rough area rug with her toe, lost in her own worried thoughts. She hated asking for help and hated, even more, admitting that she was scared. But she really was scared, and Mimi was the only person—for lack of a better word—who was around to talk. Andrew and Chris had left weeks ago for Mississippi to stay at Chris's mother's house, and Michele had returned to Haiti to visit family.

"I see. I'm sorry that work has been

sporadic. Is there another job that you could do or an employer you could contact?" asked Mimi, stubbing the smoldering butt out on the non-existent floor at her feet.

"No. No tourists are visiting now so most places are closed, at least temporarily. I don't know how to do other work outside of service industry stuff, and there's nothing available right now."

"Well, it seems that you have two options then," replied Mimi as she stood up and smoothed her housecoat over her knees. "Learn to do something else or go where there is some work."

"Go?" Ashlynne asked bewilderedly.

"Yes, Dear. Go. If the work you do is for tourists and there are no tourists in New Orleans this summer, then go where there are summer tourists. Really, Ashlynne, it's simple," sighed Mimi. "I think if you had done more thinking and less worrying you would have come up with a solution yourself much earlier, but I'm glad to have been of help."

Ashlynne narrowed her eyes at the retreating form of the spirit as it walked further into the mist and away from the mirror's opening. Mimi's tone was definitely condescending, but Ashlynne knew she was right. She had worried herself into a corner rather than thinking about her options.

"Clarity from a mirror," she chuckled to herself. "It's fitting, I guess. C'mon Murphy, it's time for bed."

As she drifted off into a fitful sleep, Mimi's words reverberated in her mind, and images of clear blue waters, quaint downtown shopping areas, and picture-perfect lighthouses flashed like hundreds of postcards behind her closed eyelids.

"Go where the summer tourists are," she mumbled to Murphy who was already fast asleep in a pile of blankets at her feet.

Chapter 2

Murphy nudged Ashlynne, pushing his cold nose into the bend of her elbow. Startled awake, she shot him a bleary-eyed glare as she swung her legs out of bed and breathed in the scent of the coffee that had brewed while she slept. She yawned and tried to gather her thoughts as the small dog hopped down with more enthusiasm than his mistress and pranced to the back door where he sat waiting to be let out into the courtyard.

Ashlynne stumbled into the kitchen, cracked open the back door for the dog, and shuffled into the tiny bathroom. As she washed her hands, she caught sight of her reflection and grimaced; dark circles and a splotchy complexion spoke volumes about the stress, lack of sleep, and anxiety that had plagued her for weeks. Yawning, she splashed cold water onto her face, slathered on lotion, and stepped back into the kitchen for her coffee. She knew there were plans with a capital P to be decided upon, but nothing was going to be accomplished before coffee.

Murphy had slipped back in through the propped door and was waiting for his breakfast. Shooting him a withering glance she muttered, "Wait your turn. Just let me have a sip before we tackle food and cookies, please."

Murphy laid down with a barely audible grumble that Ashlynne chose to ignore as she poured the coffee into her mug and added the cream. Letting the fragrant ambrosia begin to clarify her blurry thoughts, she stretched both arms over her head and felt the muscles in her shoulders pop and crack.

As the sun rose over the banana trees that

ringed the courtyard outside of the back door, Ashlynne Barrow sipped her coffee and watched Murphy inhale his breakfast of canned pumpkin mixed with kibble. Her thoughts arrived quickly and furiously, and she could feel the familiar anxiety slithering in to wrap itself around her, constricting and choking her into a standstill.

"Nope!" She jumped to her feet, tossing Murphy his after-breakfast cookie, and she strode with purpose into the bedroom and yanked the coverlet back into place over the pillows.

"Go where the summer tourists are! You know where this is. You know what you have to do. It's best to just be about it, Ashlynne," she lectured herself out loud as she pulled a pair of faded Levi's up over her hips and jammed her feet into a pair of disreputable flip-flops. She swapped out a tank top for the t-shirt she had slept in and braided her long red hair over one shoulder. Purposely avoiding her reflection in the bathroom mirror while brushing her teeth, she watched the water from the tap swirl its way down the sink and into the drain. Mentally, she watched it travel through the ancient pipes and into the decaying sewers of her neighborhood. Ashlynne cranked the faucet off, wiped her mouth, and returned to the kitchen to pour another cup of coffee.

Gathering her laptop, the coffee, and her phone, Ashlynne went to sit in the courtyard that she shared with her landlord and readied herself for a morning of planning. Planning with a capital P.

For Ashlynne, 'going where the summer tourists are' meant one thing: North. Back to where she came from. She hesitated to call it home because she had never really had a home until she came to New Orleans. But she came here from up north, specifically Northern Michigan, and it looked like the 'plan with a capital P' was to return.

Northern Michigan is a summer tourist and resort mecca for the Midwestern states and for Florida's snowbirds. The picturesque small towns that dotted the edges of the northwesternmost edge of the mitten-shaped state drew families from Michigan's more industrial and populated southern regions as well as affluent visitors from Chicago and its suburbs. While Northern Michigan also homes ski resorts and winter lodges, it is the summer season that makes the area so popular with vacationers. For those that live there year-round, most of the local jobs involve catering to those visitors in one way or another. Because of this, Ashlynne opened the largest online classified page of regional jobs that she could find and began scanning the listings. She needed not only a job but one that provided room and board —and would allow her to bring Murphy along. She knew it was a long shot but decided to dedicate the morning to her hunt.

Sipping her coffee and scrolling through the assorted job listings, Ashlynne spent a not-too-terrible morning in the courtyard. Though nothing had been decided yet, having the basics of a plan did wonders for the anxiety that plagued her for the past few months. As the sun rose to its zenith, Ashlynne flipped past job offers for baristas, servers, bartenders, and floral assistants. While these were all jobs she could do, the pay was low and there was no housing available. Just as she was getting ready to give up entirely, a listing for 'house manager' caught her attention. Hoping it wasn't for a handyman—a job she absolutely wasn't qualified for—she clicked on the link and read the description:

Large estate interviewing for a House Manager for the summer season. Duties include facilitating housekeepers as well as scheduling gardeners and any needed maintenance. Estate is offered to private guests and groups, and the House Manager is responsible for guests' comfort with morning coffee and pastries being set in the kitchen, wine and cheeses offered in the evenings, turn-down services for the bedrooms, and fresh linens provided daily. Room and board, as well as salary, will be provided. Please reply with the information requested below to be considered.

Ashlynne read and re-read the listing. It was absolutely perfect for what she needed and because of that, she was immediately skeptical.

"What do you think, Murphy?" she asked her dog who was lounging in the sun, the ghost of her landlord's long-dead poodle sitting by his side. Murphy sighed, adjusted his position into a shadier spot, and went back to sleep.

"Well, not much to lose in applying, I suppose." Ashlynne hit 'reply' to take her to her email page and began typing out the information required to apply for the position. She hit the send button with a determined click on the keyboard and closed the laptop with satisfaction. She wasn't sure what would come from the application, but she felt better for having taken some action to get her out of the difficult situation she had been stuck in. Standing up and gathering her empty coffee cup, laptop, and phone, she called to the dog and ushered him into the house ahead of her. She tossed him a cookie and opened the fridge to see what she could put together for lunch. What she wanted was a huge plate of thin fried catfish—her favorite dish offered by one of the few chain restaurants located in the Quarter. But that required money, and she didn't have any to spare for take-out. Instead, she made a salad. With a sigh, she pulled lettuce, carrots, and cucumbers from the crisper. Further back, she found the last of some Parmesan cheese and a handful of strawberries. She drizzled a portion of dressing over the bowl-full of veggies and fruit and sat down at the table to check her text messages. She hoped to see something from Andrew, but there was nothing new under his name. With a sigh, she dug into her salad and tried to pretend it was catfish with no luck whatsoever.

Ashlynne rinsed her bowl, set it beside her coffee cup to wash later, and decided it was time to get out of the house. She clipped the leash to Murphy's harness and followed him out the front door, locking it securely behind her. Rolling one shoulder and then the other, Ashlynne released the tension that had been locked there and set out to enjoy her beloved neighborhood. If this job came through, she wouldn't be back for a long while, a thought that made her heart hurt.

The owl sat almost hidden within the branches of the large lime tree across from the redhead's house. Its massive head swiveled as it watched the young woman exit with the dog and make her way further into the New Orleans neighborhood, blinking its dirty yellow eyes to avoid the brilliant light that played about her head. The owl had been sent on similar errands to observe humans that had drawn its mistress's interest, but it had never seen one that sparkled and shone like this one; she just might be able to help. With a screech that sent the neighborhood cats running to cower beneath the houses, the massive bird of prey took flight, soaring high over the block and into the mist that gathered on the northern horizon.

Chapter 3

Pulling through a pile of t-shirts, Ashlynne tried—

unsuccessfully—to whittle down a wardrobe that would be suitable for the summer up north. Though it had been several years since she had been there, she had little difficulty recalling the drastic temperature changes that occurred that close to Lake Michigan; mornings could dawn at a bracing fifty degrees with the late afternoon bringing in bright sunshine and eighty-five, and the sunset's evening air and lake breezes could have you scrambling for a sweater once again. Aside from trying to pull together enough light sweaters and shorts, she found herself at a complete loss as to what attire a House

Manager should wear.

"Are there office hours, do you think, Murph?" she asked the small terrier who sat watching as the piles of clothes grew and diminished only to grow again on a different spot of the bed.

"I wish the email had provided a few more instructions aside from when to show up," continued Ashlynne as she chose a lightweight cotton sweater to bring along.

Two days after submitting her email application, Ashlynne received a response from the job recruitment site on behalf of the owner of Rosehaven. The email welcomed her as the summer House Manager, provided her salary information, and asked for Murphy's veterinarian's name and phone number to verify his up-to-date shots and vaccinations. Once she provided that information—as well as her bank's direct deposit details—the only other information she received was the date she was to arrive at the property, directions, and a receipt for the first month's pay deposited into her bank account.

"I guess we'll have more instructions and information once we get there," she said to the dog as she added a pair of black cropped pants and several conservative blouses to the pile designated for work. Surveying the three piles—work, days off, and sweaters—she felt confident that she had all she would need and gathered the cast-offs to return to a drawer or hanger.

Ashlynne laid the open suitcase on the floor at the foot of her bed, ready to have last-minute toiletries and her Tarot cards added in the morning before zipping it closed for the almost 2-day bus trip north.

"It's almost dinner time, Murphy. This day has just flown by! I'll be right back and get you settled. I just need to pay Mr. Alvin the rent for the summer so we have a home to come back to in September." Ruffling the dog's wiry fur that sprouted like unruly weeds around the key-shaped mark on his forehead, Ashlynne grabbed the envelope of cash that would secure her New Orleans home in her absence and stepped out her front door. Two steps to her right and she stood on her landlord's stoop where she dropped the envelope through the mail slot. Mr. Alvin was expecting it and promised to drop her receipt for her advanced rental payment through the mail slot on her side. She had no reason whatsoever to doubt him. She was hit again with a twinge of pain in her chest at the thought of leaving this place that had become home.

"It's only for the summer, Ash. Just a few short weeks and the money is amazing. You can come back here, and even if it's still slow you'll have enough to live on until Christmas."

Ashlynne stepped back into her front room and surveyed the space. She had vacuumed, set her houseplants out into the courtyard to be kept alive with a combination of sub-tropical rains and Mr. Alvin's sporadic care, and draped cotton sheets over her sofa and armchair to keep any errant mice from the furniture's upholstery. In the morning she would cover her bed the same way and finish cleaning out her refrigerator. The few non-perishables that remained in the cupboards would keep while she was gone.

From the mirror came a friendly voice, "It looks like you're preparing nicely."

"Hi, Mimi. Yeah, I'm almost done. Oh, hey! Do I need to cover your mirror or anything?" she asked the spirit within the glass.

"No, Dear. I don't hold any special claim to this mirror, or any mirror as far as that's concerned. I don't even need a mirror to talk to you, but it is the easiest way for us to both see each other."

"OK, I just wanted to make sure. I'll be gone for a while." Try as she might, the nervousness and sadness of leaving New Orleans crept into her voice and was not at all lost on Mimi.

"You will be fine, Dear. As you said, there is no work here right now, so you go where the work is. The job you've acquired will be perfectly suited for your skills, and when you need me, I'm sure there is no small number of mirrors that you can use to call on me," the spirit assured Ashlynne.

Something about her tone of voice caused a ripple of trepidation to roll down Ashlynne's spine, and she looked sharply up at Mimi.

"What do you mean? Is there something about this job that I need to know?" she asked, her voice rising at the last word and giving away her fear.

"It is like I said, Dear. This job will be perfectly suited to your skills," and Mimi sauntered off beyond the left of the mirror's frame.

Ashlynne watched the mirror for a few

more seconds hoping that Mimi would return, but the glass remained empty save for the reflection of her living room. She knew she could call her back but doubted the spirit would give her any more information than the cryptic message already imparted, so she didn't bother.

She grabbed the drawstring bag holding her Tarot cards and crystal point and set them on top of her clothes in the suitcase. Digging around in her tote, she located the Hag—or Holey—stone that served as her incense holder. Cradling the nondescript stone in her hand, Ashlynne thought back to when she and Andrew had discovered its true powers, that stones such as these allowed those without the Sight to see what the psychic could naturally observe: Faeries, thin spaces, and ghosts. Missing Andrew anew, she added the stone to her suitcase as well as a sweater for Murphy and zipped the suitcase closed. She stowed the tote in her bedroom closet and wheeled the suitcase into the living room, leaving it by the front door.

After checking her phone and seeing that the radio silence continued from Andrew, despite her last several texts detailing her summer plans, she decided to get herself and the dog fed so she could get some rest before they left for the bus stop in the morning. Four o'clock would come fast.

Murphy wolfed down his dinner while Ashlynne grilled a sandwich of ham and Swiss that not only smelled great but managed to use up the last of the ham, the cheese, the bread, and the butter.

Adding the last handful of grapes to the plate and pouring a glass of the last of the orange juice had her feeling quite virtuous. The refrigerator now held a lone apple, some cream to be used in her coffee in the morning, and some lettuce that had seen better days. She cut the apple up for Murphy, threw the lettuce away, bagged the garbage, and deposited it in one of the cans lined up along the outside of the duplex. Mr. Alvin would continue to take them to the road weekly, so that was one more task out of the way before she left in the morning.

Try as she might to find another task, there was nothing left to do at the end of her last night in her little apartment. She let Murphy inside from his evening constitutional, clicked off the kitchen light, and moved into her bedroom. Seeing it all with the perspective that 'this is the last time I'll be here for months,' she smiled at the homey space she had created for herself against all odds. Her bed, piled high with a down comforter and pillows of blue and white, welcomed her to sleep no matter how long or exhausting her day had been. The filmy white curtains that hung at the window behind her headboard filtered the seeping light and played homage to the idea of curtained beds that were most popular long ago. This was her refuge, and she would miss it terribly.

Ashlynne climbed into bed and set the alarm on her phone to sound at four o'clock in the morning. After confirming her taxi for a four-thirty pick-up, she switched off the bedside lamp and lay quietly, listening to the soft hum of the air conditioner. Her eyelids grew heavy, and she drifted off into a fitful sleep full of half-formed dreams about lost suitcases and missed bus connections. The only constant through the jumble of images and disjointed scenarios was the large owl that watched from a rooftop or tree branch, its dirty yellow eyes were unblinking and cold.

Chapter 4

The alarm sounded loudly next to Ashlynne's ear, startling her out of a deep sleep full of anxious, disjointed dreams.

Groaning, she threw the covers back, slid out of bed, and pulled on the clothes she had laid out the night before for her trip. Murphy had not moved a muscle and slept like a furry lump beneath the blankets she had tossed on top of him on her way out of bed. Deciding to let him be, she shuffled into the bathroom to brush her teeth and splash water on her face in a desperate attempt to wake up. It didn't work.

Coffee would do it. She poured cream into her mug, added the hot brew on top, and took a long, restorative drink that flowed through her foggy brain and heavy limbs. Feeling almost human, Ashlynne clapped her hands together sharply to summon the still-sleeping dog from the bed. She watched in amusement as he walked slowly by, shooting her a sideways glance full of sleepy annoyance on his way to the open back door.

"Now you know how it feels. Don't you, Murph?" Ashlynne chuckled at the small dog as he headed out into the still-dark morning.

"Breakfast is coming right up, though—don't you worry!" she assured him as she spooned the last of the canned pumpkin into his bowl, mixing the kibble in after it.

"Here, Murphy—come eat!" she called out the door, leaving it propped open for him so she could go make the bed, wash the last of the dishes, and set the timers on the front room lamps. The taxi would be here soon to take them both to the bus station. Her heart twinged again at the thought of not only leaving her home but returning to a place that didn't hold many good memories. Cold and gray winters, state-run juvenile group homes, and abuses both large and small had all sent her traveling a path south as soon as she was old enough to slip away. Crash-landing in New Orleans turned out to be both fortuitous and a blessing beyond anything she had ever thought she deserved. Returning to the setting of her miserable childhood scared her more than she had realized during the relative excitement of the planning stages of leaving for the summer months. Facing it full-on, with only ten minutes before the taxi arrived, took all her strength to not cancel the whole thing and take her chances in the empty city of New Orleans.

Ashlynne squared her shoulders and resolutely finished making the bed before switching off the bedside lamp. She grabbed her phone charger and stowed it in her backpack. She was just clipping Murphy's leash onto his harness when the taxi beeped its horn outside the front door. Taking a deep breath, she hoisted her backpack over one shoulder, pulled the telescoping handle out of her suitcase, and looped Murphy's leash around her wrist. Giving her home one last glance, she pushed open the front door, stepped out into the heavy morning air, and locked the door behind her. As the taxi pulled away, she and Murphy both watched their apartment grow smaller and smaller in the rear window of the cab as it sped toward the bus station, the first step of their summer adventure.

Murphy curled up on Ashlynne's lap during the short ride, made even shorter by the utter lack of traffic. Knowing she had made the right decision to leave for a few months didn't quell the sadness of seeing her city so deserted.

The taxi pulled into the drop-off zone of the bus station, and the driver lifted her suitcase from the trunk. She handed over the amount indicated for the ride plus a tip, grabbed the dog's leash and her backpack, and walked through the front doors of the dingy bus station lobby to find her boarding instructions.

The lobby was as deserted as the streets outside of its grimed-over glass doors, so finding the one and only cashier working at five in the morning wasn't difficult. She gently stepped over a man sprawled out on the dirty floor tiles; he was still clutching a hand-lettered sign asking for money with a 'God Bless' squeezed in as an obvious after-thought. Ashlynne and Murphy made their way to the only lit ticket booth hoping the woman working was friendlier than she appeared to be. She handed her ticket receipt and ID through the half-circle opening in the scratched plexiglass barrier. The cashier grunted something indistinguishable in Ashlynne's direction, shoved her ID back at her, stapled a boarding pass to her receipt, and sent the documents skittering back through the plexiglass opening. Barely catching her documents before they flew off the short counter and onto the filthy floor, Ashlynne shot the surly woman a sour look and walked toward the outside benches to wait for her bus to arrive.

"Looks certainly aren't deceiving, are they Murph?" she whispered to her four-legged companion as he trotted alongside her and out into the early morning light.

The two of them took a seat on one of the deserted benches and settled in to wait for the bus's arrival. It was now a quarter past five in the morning, and the day's light started to creep up over the houses and commercial buildings' roofs that lay just outside the parking lot. Birds began to call and cry to each other, and the feral cats that had roamed the streets all night hunting rats and mice could be seen slinking back along the edges of buildings to their hidey-holes in cracked foundations, empty buildings, and overgrown city lots.

As she watched the city awaken in the brightening dawn, the benches began to fill up with passengers waiting to board the bus. She saw several people around her age dressed in trendy, disheveled rags that were probably ridiculously expensive, a woman who looked to be in her late thirties typing rapidly on her phone, an elderly man who seemed unsure of where he was, and a purple-haired teen who sat snoozing—her backpack jammed securely between her knees. These were the passengers who were living. Ashlynne could also see spirits that, for whatever reason, remained here at the bus station after their physical death. She quietly observed the spirit of a young boy holding a basketball and wearing a dark green baseball cap. Then her attention shifted to a middle-aged businessman whose tragic death became obvious when he turned to look at Ashlynne, revealing half of his face to be a mangled mess of flesh, blood, and bone. Pieces of asphalt were stuck in the wound and littered around the front of his suit coat. She smiled gently in his direction and watched as he turned at the sound of the approaching bus. He stood and slowly faded out of view as he walked toward the on-coming vehicle—an endless, repeating loop of his demise.

The living began to stir and gather their belongings as the bus stopped with a screech and hiss from its air brakes. The driver swung down from his seat and opened the storage compartments under the bus. Ashlynne stowed her wheeled suitcase in the compartment nearest to the back and boarded the bus carrying her backpack over her shoulder and holding Murphy under one arm. She presented her ticket information to the driver—including the extra seat she was required to purchase for her dog—and scooted sideways down the narrow center aisle until she located their seats. Setting Murphy down by the window and taking the center seat for herself, she sent up a silent prayer that the aisle seat would remain empty.

As the other passengers boarded and located their places, Ashlynne pulled her earphones from the front pocket of her bag and opened the music app on her phone. She pulled snacks for both her and the dog to the top of the bag in case they should get hungry before the bus reached the next stop with a restaurant nearby.

The driver's softly accented voice, more Georgia than New Orleans, informed the bus's occupants that they would be departing shortly. The driver read off the various stops and transfers they would be making. Ashlynne tuned it all out, flipped through her playlists, and finally settled on a variety of Blues artists, knowingly picking at the emotional wound of leaving New Orleans.

With a sigh, she settled back, closed her eyes, and let the deep velvet tone of B.B. King's iconic voice wrap itself around her heart and soul. The bus pulled out of the station and set its course north.

Chapter 5

The bus lumbered down the road, bumping and banging over New Orleans' cratered streets until it entered the morning rush of traffic on the highway and headed to Baton Rouge for the first of the scheduled transfers. With barely a dent in the trip, Ashlynne didn't plan on getting breakfast or snacks on the first stop, opting instead to take Murphy out for a quick potty break before climbing onto the next bus that would carry them further north and further from home.

As the sun rose high in the achingly blue sky, the gentle rocking of the bus and the songs of B.B. King, Etta James, John Lee Hooker, and Muddy Waters lulled her into a semi-sleep through the state of Mississippi. Hours later as the sun began its descent, she was roused for dinner at a truck stop outside of Memphis by the hissing of the bus's air brakes and a blood-pumping rendition of "Preachin' Blues" by Larkin Poe. Ashlynne stood, stretched, and took a deep breath trying to clear the fogginess that had settled in over the last twelve hours. It was now seven forty-five in the evening, and New Orleans was firmly in her mind's rearview mirror. This stop included a bus transfer with time to eat at the small cafe attached to the parking lot, and Ashlynne planned on taking advantage of the break in the schedule to take Murphy for a walk, stretch her legs, and get some dinner for the two of them. She clipped the dog's leash to his harness, slung her backpack over one shoulder, and sidled down the narrow aisle to the open double doors that deposited them into the stadium-bright parking lot. As she walked Murphy toward

the patch of grass marked 'Dog Run,' the
gathering twilight of the evening outside of
the harshly lit parking area wrapped them
both in the soft, spring air of the Tennessee
evening. Murphy nosed around collecting the
scents of the new place, and Ashlynne took a
deep breath of the fresh air, beginning to feel
a bit more awake.

"C'mon, Murphy," she said to the small
terrier who was currently shoulder-deep in
the roadside flora, breathing deeply the scents
of discarded fast-food cartons, lost shoes, and
the possums and raccoons that scavenged the
area.

"My stomach is growling. Let's go find
some dinner."

They wandered back to the cafe and
stopped short at the sign on the door stating
in no uncertain terms that dogs were not
allowed inside. Kicking herself for forgetting
that not everywhere was as dog friendly as
New Orleans, Ashlynne called the phone

number on the cafe's sign and ordered a cheese omelet, hash browns, toast, and a large coffee with cream for take-out. She paid by card over the phone and settled herself and the dog on the bench outside to wait for their dinner.

Ten minutes later, the cafe's door swung open and a young boy who looked to be one of the dishwashers plunked a take-out container next to her along with a large cup of coffee and a napkin.

"Is there cream in the coffee?" she asked him as he turned to go back inside.

Grunting something in her direction but not making eye contact, the boy fished two packets of powdered creamer out of his apron pocket, dropped them on her take-out box, and retreated into the cafe.

Grimacing at the packets, Ashlynne muttered, "Gross. I should have ordered a small milk if this is what they call cream," resolutely sprinkling the offending powder into her coffee.

"Is it powdered cleanser or is it powdered cream? Nobody knows…" she said sarcastically to Murphy who was much more interested in the take-out container's contents than his human's irritation with the lack of half-and-half for her coffee.

"Fine, we'll eat," she said and opened the container, motioning the dog.

"Well, crap. This just gets better and better, doesn't it?" grumbled Ashlynne as she eyed the contents of the container. There were no hash browns but instead grits with a blob of too-yellow margarine in the center, instead of toast there was a biscuit that was baked sometime around 1972, and no jelly.

Deciding that it was not worth the trouble to ask the cafe to fix her order, she carefully separated the Styrofoam container's lid from the side holding the food and scooped some of the now-gelatinous grits, a third of the omelet-cut into bite-sized bits, and part of the biscuit into it and set it all in front of the dog.

"Happy?" she asked, and he wolfed down the breakfast, not caring one bit if it contained grits instead of potatoes and margarine instead of butter. Having lived on the streets for more time than he wanted to think about, Murphy knew the value of eating what was available and making the best of it. He'd certainly eaten worse than this, that's for sure.

Ashlynne added a generous amount of salt and pepper to her portion of the omelet and ate it as fast as possible before the temperature could cool any further. It wasn't terrible but it wasn't great, and she was happy to wash it down with the strong coffee that was made stronger by the lack of real cream or milk available. Still hungry, she eyed the grits, decided she just couldn't do it, and scooped them into Murphy's empty container top. She dug around in her pack, found a granola bar, and munched on it while watching the customers flow in and out of the cafe. By the looks on their faces, she surmised that the food eaten within wasn't much better than what was sent out in Styrofoam.

Murphy finished his food and was beginning to pull and tug at the leash, so Ashlynne threw away the detritus of the meal and the cream-colored coffee and stood up. This allowed Murphy to lead the way as he nosed around in the grassy area again. She was happy to let the little dog get some exercise before they boarded the new bus to begin the next leg of the trip north.

As Murphy continued his exploration of the parking lot's rubbish, Ashlynne could see that boarding was beginning and lead him back onto the pavement. His one attempt at resistance proved futile in the face of his human, so he allowed himself to be walked back to the hated bus where the smells gathered like wet wool, leaving him feeling choked and smothered. Raising his small head, the curious key-shaped scar between his eyes clearly visible in the brightly lit parking lot, Murphy took a last deep breath of fresh air full of gently flowing scents before entering the confined space of the bus.

Ashlynne bent down and scooped Murphy up, holding him under one arm as she navigated her way down the center aisle looking for an empty row of seats. This bus was not as full as the original departure from New Orleans, and she had her pick of available spaces. She chose a short row of two seats located at the back of the bus and settled them both into place just as the bus's doors swung shut and the lights dimmed within. She pulled a hooded sweatshirt from her pack and slipped it on. Lifting Murphy onto her lap, Ashlynne settled in for the overnight trip. As the bus pulled out, swaying gently, Murphy's comforting weight on her lap helped lull her back into a state just outside of sleep where ideas, images, and words flowed into her mind then back out again—a river of half conceived impressions and thoughts.

As the big bus lumbered its way north and west, Ashlynne spent the night alternately snoozing, listening to music, and playing games on her phone. It was during one of the moments spent playing games that the phone chimed to alert her to a text.

Andrew: *Hey, my baby, where you at?*

Ashlynne smiled and chuckled quietly—finally! A message from Andrew! She missed him so much and hated making her summer-away plans without him.

Ashlynne: *Hey there, yourself! I'm on a big ole' ugly bus headed north. I miss you!*

Andrew: *North? Why? Where's Murphy? Why didn't you tell me???*

Ashlynne scowled at the phone.

Ashlynne: *I did tell you! Check your messages! Murphy's with me. I'll be back in September and Mr. Alvin has my rent. There's no work right now—I needed to get a job and this opportunity sounds amazing! I'll fill you in later.*

Andrew's reply came a few seconds later—

Andrew: *OK, Chris and I will be back home in a few weeks or so, just finishing up some things at his mom's place. Let me know when you get to wherever you're going. 'North' isn't very specific, Ash.*

Thumbs flying over the phone's keyboard, Ashlynne typed out her reply and hit send:

Ashlynne: *Hug Chris for me. I'm going to Charlevoix in Michigan to manage a lakefront estate.*

Ashlynne laughed out loud at the final reply in the thread—

Andrew: *Well, aren't you fancy?*

The sun began to rise, brightening the sky little by little as Ashlynne and Murphy hit the first twenty-four hours of their summer away from home. Chicago's skyline loomed large as the bus pulled into an expansive parking lot with numerous bays, glaringly lit in the still-gray dawn.

Ashlynne and Murphy followed the rest of their traveling companions out into the chilly, Midwestern morning air that was so different from the soft warmth of their southern stops. This air was sharp and crisp with a bracing breeze that smelled of the waters of Lake Michigan.

She let Murphy do his business in the patchy grass just to the right of a bank of vending machines, walking over to see what the offerings were once he had finished. Wistfully turning away from the so-called coffee offered in one of the machines, knowing she would only be disappointed in whatever hot mess was being sold from within, she opted instead for a plastic bottle of Coca-Cola and a bag of crackers. The soda would fulfill her desperate need for caffeine, and the crackers she could share with Murphy until their next stop.

Boarding the next bus proved that the luxury of not sharing a row of seats was over for the time being as she squeezed her way past row after row of feet, bags, and purses. She headed to the very back where Ashlynne and Murphy managed to slide past an older businessman, seated on the aisle, and they wiggled into the two seats next to him—one in the middle and one at the window. Ashlynne pretended to ignore the withering look that her dog gave her as she deposited him between her and the businessman and sat down at the window.

As the bus pulled away making its way out of Illinois, Ashlynne shared the bag of crackers with Murphy and watched the scenery change outside the bus's dirty window. Spring was a gray and cold affair here and would only grow grayer and colder the further north they traveled. Shying away from that depressing fact, Ashlynne bunched her pack up between her head and the window, put her earbuds back in, gathered Murphy onto her lap, and closed her eyes to better let the sounds of Clapton's raspy voice lull her back into semi-consciousness.

Ashlynne and Murphy stayed this way until the bus stopped at a station in Grand Rapids, Michigan where they ate a not-too-terrible lunch in a diner that didn't mind allowing the dog inside. They wandered a bit and checked out the small gift shop stocked with University of Michigan and Michigan State University logos emblazoned on everything from beer cozies to sweatshirts to baseball caps.

Ashlynne watched as their bags were transferred from the bus she had exited earlier to another, smaller, bus with an illuminated sign that said CHARLEVOIX.

"Well, Murph, this is it! The last leg of our trip—next stop is Charlevoix."

As Ashlynne settled into the nearly deserted bus, emblazoned with the head of a Native American Chief, she couldn't help but feel a little excited. Knowing that Andrew and

Chris weren't going to be home for several more weeks helped a little; she would be missing them whether she had stayed home or left. While she hadn't spent a lot of time in the city of Charlevoix as a kid, she remembered it as quaint, picturesque, and charming in the summer months. It wasn't called "Charlevoix the Beautiful" for no reason. She watched as the skyline of Grand Rapids moved out of view and the endless rolling fields of rural farmland in the center of the mitten state stretched out ahead of them, soon to give way to the unbroken expanse of Lake Michigan's deep blue waters.

Chapter 6

With a screech and a hiss, the bus stopped in a tiny parking lot that faced a small inland lake, housing a marina that was a third of the way filled with boats of all sizes and types. Through the bus's window, Ashlynne spied huge multi-stateroom yachts moored side by side with small sailboats, commercial fishing boats, and the occasional sleek speedboat thrown in for good measure. While the season had not yet officially begun, many of the affluent second-home owners seemed to already be in residence.

"Let's go, Murph, we're here," she said, nudging the snoozing dog curled up on the seat next to her.

Murphy stretched and yawned and leaned around her to look out the window. With a bored glance back over his shoulder at the scene outside, he jumped down into the aisle and waited for the leash to be clipped to his harness so they could exit the bus. Murphy had enough—he wanted food, a place to go to the bathroom, and a good, brisk walk. The bus, with its cloyingly humid interior and fetid smell, was something he hoped to not get back into for a very long while.

Ashlynne gathered her backpack, clipped Murphy's leash to his harness, and nudged the antsy dog along the aisle ahead of her. They stood behind the other four passengers that were disembarking; they all seemed distracted thinking of their next location, be it a family's home, the large green and white ferry that would take them two hours over the lake to tiny Beaver Island or waiting for the next bus that would take them further north into Michigan's Upper Peninsula. Loneliness crept up on her as she moved down the aisle to the open bus doors. She wished that she were more confident in where she was going and what she would be doing. For the moment, though, she was operating on the barest of knowledge with no one to talk to or guide her.

"Just like how I felt when I left here, Murphy," she said to her one and only companion as she followed him to a grassy area where he could relieve himself.

"There is something to be said for coming full circle, I suppose," she continued as the dog nudged a pinecone with his nose, inhaling its scent deeply.

Letting Murphy wander on a long leash, Ashlynne rummaged through her backpack for the envelope that had arrived in her mailbox back in New Orleans a week before she left. Slipping the folded paper out to read it for the thousandth time, she was hoping the instructions within would mean more to her now that she was in Charlevoix.

Ashlynne,

Thank you for accepting the position of House Manager for Rosehaven Cottage. We are confident that you will be a perfect fit for the house. The street number is on the key that is enclosed and will unlock the service entrance to the left of the front porch. Keys to the main front doors and all interior doors are at the house with additional property information. Please let yourself in and make yourself at home. The homeowner will be out of the country for the duration of the summer, so the house will be unoccupied at your arrival.

Regards,

Landmark Realty on behalf of:

Rosehaven Cottage, LLC

Michigan Avenue

Charlevoix

Ashlynne tipped the envelope upside down and allowed the heavy brass key to fall into her hand. Slipping the notecard back into the envelope, she dropped it into her backpack and held the key up to better see the number stamped into it. 1102. Ashlynne opened the map application on her phone and keyed in the address for Rosehaven.

"It's only about three blocks from here, Murphy. Feel like a walk? I hope so because I don't think we'll find a taxi here," she added with a rueful chuckle as she looked around at the utterly deserted parking lot. Her suitcase sat on the sidewalk in front of the Ferry Terminal looking lost and lonely. Shaking her head after considering how this was a place where entire suitcases could sit unattended and not be stolen, she tugged on Murphy's leash to signal it was time to go.

Thrilled to hear there would be a walk, the small terrier pranced along beside Ashlynne as she pulled the wheeled suitcase over rutted and broken sidewalks toward the drawbridge that divided the town in half. The very act of lugging the suitcase over bumps and holes was so much like pulling her tote home after a night reading cards in Jackson Square that she had to stop and catch her breath. Her chest constricted painfully as she physically reacted to the sudden onset of homesickness, and her eyes burned with unshed tears. The silence of the tiny city was deafening.

"It's only just now eight o'clock, and there is absolutely no one out on the street. No people are out walking, there's no music, there are no open shops anywhere," she whispered sadly to her dog.

Murphy's head tilted right on cue; it was such a fantastical addition to her Wizard of Oz moment that she couldn't help but laugh, though there was a sharp edge of hysteria to it.

"We're not in Kansas anymore, Murphy!" Ashlynne proclaimed with a wave of her arm that encompassed the whole of the silent downtown. And with that unexpected brevity, the moment of panic—if not the homesickness—passed and Ashlynne resumed her walk to the house that would be her home for the next several months.

Crossing the draw bridge to the north side of town, Ashlynne and Murphy followed the sidewalk up Michigan Avenue and into its quietly elegant interior. Large homes dating from the early 1900s with perfectly manicured lawns sat well back from the sidewalk, shaded by 300-hundred-year-old maples and oaks. A few of the houses still had boarded windows and empty porches—not yet opened for the summer season, though most had their expansive wrap-around porches outfitted with white wicker furniture and large urns filled with red or pink geraniums. As they walked down the street, quiet in the quickly darkening sky, Murphy threw his head back and sniffed just as Ashlynne became aware of the sound of crashing waves. She stopped and peeked through the trees on the lawn of a pretty yellow house accented with crisp white columns. She spied the source of the sounds she heard and the smells that captivated her dog: Lake Michigan. She had been gone from the area just long enough to have forgotten the awesomeness of the lake; its deep blue waters and immense energy were not something she thought to miss when she had left. She knew now that she was wrong to have not given it another thought after leaving, and she sent a silent apology to the spirit of its waters.

She checked for house numbers on columns and front doors, as there were no mailboxes on the street. Ashlynne counted the numbers until she arrived at the last house on the road, nothing but trees lay beyond it.

"Here we are, Murphy," she whispered into the gathering gloom as they stood in front of an impressively large white Dutch Colonial with a swath of porch that flowed across the front of the house. Massive double front doors sat far back underneath the porch's roof with two immense second-story windows centered directly over the front doors—their softly lit glow barely piercing the shadows.

The enormity of the house took Ashlynne's breath away: the large first-floor windows, the huge porch, the second-story balconies, and finally, the third-story windows that were shuttered and dark all lined up across the front of the house and tucked under the roof's eaves like so many silent sentinels.

Two gigantic stone urns stood like guards on either side of the porch steps, each as tall as she was and filled to the brim with bright red geraniums and trailing green vines. Airy white flowers dotted the pile of red blooms, reminding Ashlynne of baby's breath in a florists' arrangement. The effect was both simple and elegant. Hanging atop the porch's waist-high railings were large Boston ferns, their foliage draping languidly in the cool evening air. Deep within the recessed porch, Ashlynne could just make out white wicker settees, rocking chairs, and sofas all dressed in perfectly faded floral chintz cushions. The architecture and decorations culminated in the effect of a Victorian summer home. What threw this effect out of whack, though, was the thin Native American man standing just to the side of the last fern at the end of the porch where its steps met the cobblestone driveway.

The man appeared to be in his late teens to early twenties. He was clad in leather pants that were laced closed just below his navel. His black hair was shaved on either side of his head with the rest left long and pulled back, tied at the nape of his neck with a leather thong. He wore a necklace of a matching length of leather that was strung through with some sort of crude pendant. The young man was bare-chested and barefooted. If he had been alive, Ashlynne would have worried that he was cold. Since he was not alive, she was more curious than worried, and she grew more curious when the lanky young man stepped sideways and winked out of view.

"Well, then! That's a neat trick, isn't it, Murphy?" exclaimed Ashlynne to the dog who was still staring at the spot on the porch where the young Native American was standing just a moment ago.

"You'll see lots of interesting things up here, Murphy. The history and memory of the land is different than in New Orleans. The spirits are pretty unique to the area if I remember correctly," she continued as she led the dog to the small side door that had to be the service entrance that her key was meant to open.

She inserted the brass key into the burnished lock, turned it, and heard a loud click as the tumblers moved within. Pushing the door open, she nudged Murphy in ahead of her and lifted her suitcase up and over the door jamb and into a small service room.

Stairs descended into darkness directly in front of her, and on the wall to her left were open wooden shelves holding equestrian riding helmets, tall leather boots, and an ancient umbrella. Further past those, steps led up to a landing where a Victorian bamboo hall tree held a bowl overflowing with assorted sunglasses and another bowl filled with different-sized pairs of winter gloves.

"How very Michigan," remarked Ashlynne as she hoisted her suitcase up and sat it next to the hall tree. Taking a deep breath, she stepped into the dark rooms to her left and followed the path of light that led her into a softly lit kitchen. Murphy trailed behind her dragging his leash along the wide-planked hardwood floor.

The kitchen opened before them, warm and glowing softly in the light of the frosted overhead lamps that were attached to several fans set almost flush with the ceiling that soared over fourteen feet above her head. The longest kitchen table Ashlynne had ever seen sat in the center of the room dividing the space between the entry where she stood and the enormous Aga Cooker and long length of marble counters on the opposite side. Six straight-backed chairs were lined up along her side of the table with two more armchairs at either end. Cabinets and cupboards galore were mounted on the walls above the counters running straight up to the ceiling. Ashlynne was sure she couldn't live enough lifetimes to accumulate all the dishes needed to fill them. The kitchen sat at the southern end of the house with large crank-open windows at the front. The other end of the room featured a stepped-down sunroom beautifully tiled with tumbled marble and crowded with large potted fig trees, hanging ferns, and overstuffed sofas. Floor-to-ceiling windows wrapped around the back and side of the kitchen, showing nothing but the inky blackness of the backyard beyond. All in all, it was the most beautiful kitchen she had ever been in and so well-appointed that the scale—easily over nine hundred square feet—felt warm and cozy rather than immense and intimidating.

"Stick close," she commanded Murphy as she unhooked his leash and placed it and her backpack on the floor next to the table. Baskets filled with fresh fruits and artisan bagels sat along the center of the table's butcher top, its surface buttery soft and oiled to a mellow sheen. In front of the baskets of fruits and loaves of bread was a black three-ring binder with the name Rosehaven scrolled across in gold lettering. Ashlynne pulled out one of the chairs and sat down as Murphy wandered into the sunroom snuffling and snorting with delight at the new array of smells.

Flipping through the pages held within the binder, Ashlynne could see a myriad of names and phone numbers—the gardener, the plumber, a grocery service, a car service, the house cleaners, laundry services, carpet cleaners, and on and on and on. It seemed as if it took the whole of Charlevoix to keep this cottage running.

Flipping back to the first page, she found a section with her name on it that detailed where her room was located and directions for using the European Aga Cooker. Deciding that the fancy oven and exploring the immense house could wait until tomorrow, she pulled a small baggie of kibble for Murphy out of her backpack and rummaged through cabinets to find a plastic bowl. It soon became apparent that plastic kitchenware did not reside in this house, so she settled on a bowl—slightly less fancy than the others—for Murphy's dog food. Adding a chopped banana from one of the baskets, Ashlynne put the bowl down for the dog and went to search for a toaster to fix herself one of the bagels.

After locating the toaster and enjoying a

bagel, Ashlynne checked her phone for messages and, seeing none, rinsed her dishes and left them in the drainer until tomorrow.

Swinging her backpack over one shoulder and retrieving her suitcase, she hoisted it up the stairs to the left of the bamboo hall tree to the second floor. The notebook had said that the House Manager's room was the first door on the left past the armoire. A small lamp perched on a dainty hall table cast a puddle of light that illuminated the door, and she gingerly turned the cut-glass doorknob and pushed the heavy wooden door open. Her 'room' was a series of rooms, a suite that had her main bedroom, a large walk-in closet, a sitting room, and a beautifully appointed bathroom with both a claw-footed tub and a modern glassed-in shower.

The bedroom faced the back of the house, directly above the kitchen's sunroom, and had its own balcony accessed by floor-to-ceiling French doors. Dropping her bags, she pulled the doors open and smiled with delight when the roar of the lake's crashing waves and the bracing breezes from its unseen shores flowed into the suite and around her.

"Isn't this lovely, Murphy?" asked Ashlynne as she turned around in time to see the small terrier hop up onto the bed and lay his head on his paws, effectively claiming his spot for the next couple of months.

"I think that's a wonderful idea! I'll be very glad to sleep in a bed tonight rather than upright in a bus seat," she chattered to her dog as she removed the numerous decorative pillows from the top of the duvet and pulled it back to reveal a soft down comforter laid over heavy cotton sheets.

"Yeah, Murph—I think we'll sleep just fine here!"

As Ashlynne pulled on a clean t-shirt and a pair of sweatpants to sleep in, a large owl landed silently on the railing of her balcony. Murphy saw it, but his low warning growl went unheard by his human as she continued to express her appreciation of their new sleeping arrangements.

Chapter 7

Ashlynne opened her eyes to the brightening sky outside of the French doors that she had left open overnight. The pines and hardwoods swayed in the mild spring breeze, and the crashing waves from the night before had turned to a gentle whisper of undulating white noise with the arrival of morning.

She stretched languidly, unbelievably comfortable under the weight of the down comforter, and checked the clock on her phone on the bedside table. Seven o'clock. With a slight groan, she bumped the still unmoving lump of a dog at her feet.

"Murphy, get up. We have a lot to do today."

The only response from the small terrier was an irritated grumble as he curled into an even tighter ball and turned his head away from her.

"Fine, have it your way," she said as she swung her legs over the side of the bed and grabbed her sweatshirt. The fresh air was invigorating and brisk as it flowed inland over the cold waters of the lake.

As Ashlynne pulled the only pair of socks she owned over her bare feet, Murphy stretched and jumped down from his nest of blankets and trotted out to the balcony. He breathed in deeply the early morning air that was scented with pine sap, green grass, and the various flowers and herbs planted in the garden below. What he didn't smell was the owl that had visited last night, and that worried him. An animal that large should have left a scent, but there was none. Murphy whined in consternation and confusion.

"What's wrong?" asked Ashlynne after

hearing the small dog's complaints.

"Come on, let's go let you out and find some coffee," she said as she headed out into the hallway. Murphy followed along, having no way to let her know what was really bothering him.

As the smell of coffee finally began to permeate the cavernous kitchen, Ashlynne's early-morning irritation, born of caffeine withdrawal and an unknown kitchen landscape, began to abate. It had taken her twenty minutes to locate the cabinet that held the coffee grounds and another five minutes to track down the coffee filters.

"What kind of crazy person keeps the coffee and the coffee filters in separate places?" she grumbled as she chopped a banana to add to the last of Murphy's kibble. Setting the bowl down on the floor she made a mental note to make a grocery list.

With a final belch of steam, the coffee maker finished its magic, and Ashlynne poured a generous amount of the half-and-half she had found in the refrigerator into an oversized white coffee mug miraculously located in the first cupboard she checked.

"Dumb luck," she mumbled as she poured the coffee in after the cream until it achieved the desired hue. Leaning against the cold marble counter, Ashlynne took a deep drink of the brew and sighed.

Murphy finished his breakfast as Ashlynne sipped her coffee. She hooked his leash to his harness and followed him out the tall French doors at the end of the sunroom and into the backyard.

Ashlynne smiled in delight at the beautiful and unexpected view that greeted them—to their right, a long columned porch matching the one on the house's front facade stretched the length of the structure. More white wicker furniture, ferns, and potted geraniums softened the outdoor living space. Delicate wrought-iron chandeliers dripping with crystals and fitted with candles hung here and there from the porch's sky-blue ceiling. Immediately in front of them, spanning the entirety of the property, was a formal knot garden crafted from expertly shaped boxwood hedges. Each opening within the knotted design held its own variety of plants making for at least a dozen individual gardens within the main horticultural structure. Dahlias, daisies, and stately snapdragons all had their own beds along with herbs such as lavender, garden sage, rosemary, and mint within their assigned places. Mounds of pink and white impatiens spiraled underneath an ornamental flowering magnolia in the garden to the far left of the flagstone walkway which ended in a crisp white arbor adorned with a climbing rose vine awaiting its summer blooms. A deep hedge of nothing but heirloom rose bushes ran the length of the porch, separated from the formal knot garden by a flagstone walkway softened by fragrant creeping thyme that grew here and there between the flat stones. At the far-right edge of the garden stood a picture-perfect gazebo perched on a small hummock and adorned with ornately planted hanging baskets of pink and white petunias. Undoubtedly, the backyard was a carefully curated space intended to look as natural and undone as possible. It was romantically magical and somewhat unsettling in its perfection.

"Oh my God," whispered Ashlynne.

She stood in her stocking feet and stared at the garden laid out before her. Turning a slow circle, she noticed a gated section next to the sunroom and led Murphy that way before he soiled the perfect flagstones.

Pleased to see a patch of grass surrounded by a border of pea-gravel that lay beyond the small gate, Ashlynne unhooked Murphy's leash and scooted him inside. She watched as he sniffed around, circled thrice, and squatted to relieve himself. Seeing that he seemed content to explore the dog run, she took a sip of her coffee and walked into the garden to take a better look.

Knowing that it was very early in the north's growing season made the sheer number of flowers and plants already showing their colors all the more incredible. The large rose garden must be a delight to the senses when it bloomed, and she imagined that this was the inspiration for the house's name.

Birds called across the crisscrossing tree limbs with a constant auditory backdrop of waves. Wondering if the lake was accessible from the property, Ashlynne took a final swallow from her coffee and set the mug on the steps of the porch. Checking to make sure that Murphy was OK, she walked to the edge of the garden to where the arbor stood with its climbing rose bushes. The lake's voice grew louder, and Ashlynne walked through the arbor following its call. Instead of an expanse of deep blue waters, she was met with a drop of cedar steps marching down a steep cliff. Deciding to take Murphy along, she returned to the dog run, clipped his harness on him, pulled her now-wet socks off, and led him back through the rose arbor.

"What do you say, boy? Up for a little early morning exploring?"

Murphy grinned up at his mistress and led the way down the steps.

Sixty-five steps down the cliff face and they stepped out into a copse of cedar trees with Lake Michigan laid out a short distance beyond.

"This just gets more amazing, doesn't it, Murph?" asked Ashlynne, picking her way around the cedar trees and stepping out onto the rock-strewn beach. Gentle waves rolled in and broke onto a vast array of colorful beach stones a few feet from where she and the dog stood. Between them and the water's edge lay a pit dug into the sand lined with large stones and containing partially charred logs.

"Oh look, Murphy! Maybe we can have evening bonfires down here!" exclaimed Ashlynne. The whole array of 'up-north summers' previously denied to her during her troubled childhood were suddenly within reach.

Murphy ranged on his long leash and gathered the scents of burnt wood, water plants, seagulls, and dead fish, constructing a scent-story of their new home. He also tried, without any luck, to catch a scent of the owl that had so far eluded him.

Feeling Ashlynne tug on his leash, he gathered in one last deep sniff of the beach and followed her back to the wooden steps that would bring them back up to the garden and the house it belonged to. The small dog, having seen and lived through so much more than most humans had, remained unsure as to whether he was completely comfortable with this new place.

"Ugh! I am so out of shape!" Ashlynne huffed as she trudged back up the cliff.

As she and the dog crested the last landing, bringing the house into view beyond the rose arbor, she froze. Murphy bumped into the back of her calves and peeked around her to see what had caused the sudden stop. Moving along the porch was a woman dressed in a breezy roaring twenties style. She seemed to be watering the ferns with a small, delicate watering can. She was slim, almost boyish in figure—as was the style of the time—and her dress complimented the blue of the porch's ceiling perfectly. The woman's dark hair was pulled back in a loose knot at the back of her head and accentuated her long neck. Ashlynne could hear the spirit humming to herself as she moved back and forth along the back porch, dripping water onto the ferns and potted geraniums.

"What do you think?" Ashlynne

whispered to Murphy, "Spirit or a memory of the house's?"

Murphy cocked his head and whined quietly.

Ashlynne closed her eyes and felt outward to the woman on the porch. Jumbled images exploded into her mind: the woman tending to an earlier version of the house's garden, a man with his hand raised in anger, another woman dressed in a housekeeper's uniform sweeping up the glass from a shattered vase, and then spiraling darkness that ended with a view of the gardens.

With a gasp, Ashlynne's eyes flew open, and she declared, "Eliza! Her name is Eliza."

Murphy watched his mistress as she grappled with her internal visions.

"Definitely a spirit, Murph. She's been with the house a long time, and I don't think she'll be any trouble. But her story doesn't seem very pleasant. She seems sad and lonesome, really."

Wandering up through the rose arbor again, Ashlynne could see that the spirit named Eliza was no longer caring for the ferns, so she and Murphy continued on their way to the top of the stairs.

"Do you think she waters the flowers every morning?" Ashlynne asked the dog as they made their way back up the flagstone walkway to the house's back doors. Meaning to take her abandoned coffee mug and discarded socks back inside, Ashlynne couldn't seem to locate the mug and finally gave up, leading the way through the French doors and into the sunroom. She unclipped Murphy from his leash and slipped his harness over his head.

"Be free!" she laughed as the small terrier ran down the length of the kitchen and skittered around the corner into the front rooms of the house, collecting scents and sounds and sights along the way.

Hoping to follow him shortly to fully

explore the large home, Ashlynne dropped the leash and harness onto a kitchen chair and placed her wet socks in the sink. Leaning over to turn off the coffee pot, her mouth dropped open in surprise and then into a delighted grin; sitting next to the coffee maker was her mug filled with fresh coffee and just the right amount of cream.

"Why, thank you, Eliza! Nice to meet you too!" laughed Ashlynne as she took a sip of the coffee and wandered off to join Murphy in his explorations.

Chapter 8

The next couple of days were spent exploring the big house, from its gabled third-floor bedrooms down to its basement level that was unlike any Michigan basement Ashlynne had ever seen. It contained a catering kitchen, an office, a gym, a tool room, the main laundry area, several storage rooms—one that was dedicated only to gift wrapping supplies! — a billiard room, a lounge with a fireplace, and the boiler room. The lower level was accessed from either a set of stairs at the side of the sunroom or from the stairs that descended directly from the service entrance where she and Murphy had originally entered the house on their first night there.

Above the basement was the main floor with its public rooms, the kitchen and sunroom, butler's pantry, formal dining room, music room, foyer, grand staircase, library, and living room.

Each room was expertly decorated with antiques and fabrics from Europe. Crystal chandeliers decadently adorned the soaring ceilings and one of a kind wool rugs, made specifically for the house, covered the dark wood floors. The top two floors were dedicated to bedrooms, most with en-suite facilities, as well as an extensive children's space on the uppermost floor. Despite the grandeur and obvious pedigree of the decor, the effect was still astonishingly comfortable, quite an accomplishment in a house with over twenty-nine rooms spanning over fifteen thousand square feet.

As Ashlynne acquainted herself with the layout—learning to move right if she was turned around, for that would eventually lead her to either the grand staircase or the smaller service stairwell—she began to relax and feel the energy within the structure. Occasionally Eliza could be felt, and she and Murphy were both delighted to encounter two small white dogs that ran and frolicked about most of the basement level. But aside from those spirits, the overall feeling was of overwhelming femaleness. There seemed to be no spirit or ghost assigned to that feeling, and Ashlynne found it very odd.

"What do you think, Murphy? Is our new home alive?" she commented in an offhand manner about a week into their stay.

Murphy emitted a low growl when the lights above their head began flickering off and on, seemingly in response to Ashlynne's question.

"Whoa...." Ashlynne whispered as she watched the light show above their heads.

The flickering lasted just long enough to notice then stopped, leaving only the bulbs shining brightly above their heads.

"Eliza? Was that you?" whispered Ashlynne.

She and Murphy waited—not sure what they expected to happen next, perhaps a bump or a thump in response. Would the lights do their flickering dance again? Would the garbage disposal start? But none of those things happened at all. It remained quiet. It was a heavy quiet, like the air before a summer storm comes in, crackling and alive yet somehow still, a space wherein anything could happen.

"I don't think I've ever met a house that is alive. Have you, Murphy?" whispered Ashlynne as she took a drink of her water.

She and Murphy were in the kitchen. He was stretched out on the floor snoozing while she was going through the house manual trying to locate the number for the grocery delivery service. She had supplemented Murphy's kibble with some canned dog food she had found in one of the cabinets, but both Ashlynne and the dog would need an infusion of food soon. She could walk to the nearest market but, unsure if they would let Murphy in and not yet comfortable enough to leave him in the house alone, the option of delivery seemed the best for now.

"Here it is," she muttered, jabbing her finger at the entry in the list of numbers associated with services that the house's inhabitants would find useful or necessary.

Pushing the number into her phone, she gave the grocery store her address, her name, and a list of items along with any acceptable substitutions should her first choices not be available. Digging around in her wallet for her debit card, she stopped in surprise when the clerk thanked her and hung up without taking payment.

"Maybe they'll run my card when they get here," she said to Murphy as she stood up to straighten the kitchen from their lunch and load the small number of dirty dishes into the dishwasher.

Ashlynne was just finishing sweeping the kitchen floor of crumbs when the bell to the service door rang.

Grabbing her debit card, she ran through the kitchen, the butler's pantry, and down the steps to the small side door and opened it for the delivery person.

A young boy stood there holding her bags emblazoned with the local market's logo; he was looking tired and bored.

"Delivery, ma'am," he stated, rather unnecessarily she thought, as she reached through the screen door propped open with her hip to take the bags from him.

"No, ma'am. I'll just put these in the kitchen for you," he drawled lazily as he pushed past her and went up the steps and turned left.

Ashlynne watched as the teen expertly maneuvered through the rooms and into the kitchen, obviously familiar with at least this part of the house. He set the bags on the expansive kitchen table, handed her the receipt, and turned to leave the way he had come in.

"Wait! I need to pay you!" cried Ashlynne, hurrying after him and waving her card in front of her.

"New here, huh?" said the boy, more a statement than a question.

"Uh, yeah," replied Ashlynne, feeling self-conscious though she wasn't sure why.

"There's an account for 1102," he said with the contempt that crops up when jaded year-round residents talk to workers new to the area.

He had a 'been-there-done-that-so-bored-I-can-hardly-stand-it' attitude that wasn't reserved exclusively to teenage workers. She had encountered it before and had probably been guilty of it herself in New Orleans. It was a response to those not yet allowed into an exclusive club, and Ashlynne knew the drill.

"Yeah, OK. Thanks for the heads-up. I appreciate it," she said, matching his bored tone and handed him a larger than necessary tip so the word got out that she would be a sympathetic and friendly addition to the summer work-force.

Murphy watched their interaction from a patch of sun on the butler's pantry rug. The social mechanizations and rituals of humans bored him. Groceries, however, did not bore him, and he decided to cut his nap short to investigate the contents of the bags.

Nosing around in each bag that Ashlynne put onto a chair to unpack, he caught the scents of the delivery boy, the cashier who had rung up the order—a smoker, and the employee who had chosen the order from the delivery order—an older woman with diabetes that she refused to treat. Murphy sat in his prettiest pose when he saw the giant butcher's bone wrapped in plastic and gave his human his best grin. It never failed to get him what he wanted, and this time was no exception. After he was given the bone, he was shooed out to the dog run to enjoy his treat in the weak spring sunshine.

Ashlynne finished unpacking the groceries in peace after moving her way-too-interested dog outside. She put items away in what she assumed were the appropriate cupboards, though try as she might, she couldn't quite remember where everything was located and she had a sinking suspicion that she probably never would.

After she stowed the plastic grocery bags in a small urn next to the French doors that lead out to the dog run (they would be perfect for cleaning up after Murphy), she sat down to check for messages from Andrew. Disappointed that there were none, she checked her email and was surprised to see one from the agency that had hired her for her current position.

Opening the email, she read quickly, her heart beating faster with anxiety.

"Well, Ash—what did you expect? That you and Murphy would just bump around all alone in this massive house all summer? This is what you were hired for, remember?" she said out loud as she made a note in the datebook provided in the house manual:

Dark Grove Enterprises
Party of 7
Arriving May 31, Checking out August 31

"I wonder what kind of business is called Dark Grove?" Ashlynne muttered as she closed the planner and went to retrieve the dog. "Maybe they're garden enthusiasts," she continued as she followed Murphy into the kitchen and opened the house manual to the section marked Guests.

"We've only got a couple of weeks before

this group arrives, Murphy. Let's see what we have to do between now and then, shall we?"

Chapter 9

The May darkness whispered its secrets in gentle splashes of waves and the calls of night-birds, and Ashlynne was awakened by light shining through the lace curtains on the French doors that separated the bedroom from the balcony beyond. Bleary-eyed, she swung her legs over the side of the tall bed, chilly toes hitting the wool rug with a barely perceivable thump. It was enough for Murphy to hear, though, and he raised his head to see what his human was up to in the middle of the night.

Following the diffused moonlight, Ashlynne pulled open the doors and stepped out into the chilly spring night.

Whispers floated on the breeze; voices

more felt than heard. The full moon sat high overhead, ringed completely in a halo of intense red.

Ashlynne shivered and wrapped her bare arms around herself.

"Red around the moon—trouble is coming," she whispered into the night air.

Murphy, having followed her outside, cocked his head at his human's voice and sat down next to her with a small whimper.

Ashlynne closed her eyes and felt outward, trying to find the source of the omen that had brought her outside. As her consciousness moved out into the night, she felt her shoulders relax and her arms drop to her sides. Her breathing deepened and slowed as she reached outward.

Where... Who...? What? Her thoughts ran into each other as she roamed the space between where she and her dog stood and the immense 'somewhere out there'. Not having a place or person to focus on left her hunting for the metaphorical needle in the haystack. Just as she was getting ready to pull back and into herself, she felt something, a ripple of energy, something not quite right. Taking a deep breath, Ashlynne moved her thoughts out further, trying to identify the anomaly that she felt. It was heavy and intense, like moving into warm, inky water, and yet it was vibrant at the same time. Seductive. As she moved closer to the darkness, electric red sparks erupted behind her eyes as she was forcibly shoved back and into her own body. Ashlynne's eyes shot open in surprise and fear as she struggled to settle herself.

"What the hell was that?" she gasped, dropping down onto one of the white wooden lounge chairs scattered around the balcony.

Murphy moved to sit as close to her as he could and leaned his head on her thigh.

She reached down to pat his head, unsure whether she was comforting him or herself and blinked rapidly trying to make rhyme or reason of what had just occurred.

"Someone knew I had found them, Murph. Someone who knows how to send back energy that gets too close."

Ashlynne stood and nudged Murphy into the house ahead of her, closing the door against the ominous moon and the whispers that floated on the wind.

Deciding that sleep was probably not going to happen again for a while, she pulled on her sweatshirt, stuffed her frozen toes into her socks, and went down to the main level to make coffee. It would be several hours before the sun's light overtook the moon's red haze, but the kitchen would be bright and comforting until then.

Curled up on the overstuffed settee in the sunroom, ensconced securely within the glow of the numerous lamps, Ashlynne and Murphy watched as the red-ringed moon moved further and further up and into the eastern sky until it was no longer visible in their westward facing windows.

Ashlynne sipped her coffee and thought about what had happened on the balcony. As always, she struggled with whether the presence she felt had anything to do with her. Over the years she had learned, oftentimes painfully, that not every sensed entity, energy, or presence had anything to do with her. Many times, she sensed these things only because she was capable of doing so and not because any action was expected or required of her.

"This feels different," she said.

Murphy raised his head and looked at her as footfalls sounded deep within the house.

"Oh, my. Everything is different about this place, isn't it?" she asked the small dog as he continued to look in the direction of the now silent footsteps.

"It's going to be hard to decide which of these things has anything to do with us, isn't it?" she continued as Murphy put his head down with a sigh.

"I don't think the Native American man or Eliza have anything to do with the presence that shot the red energy at me," Ashlynne mused aloud as she moved across the kitchen, brightening with dawn, to refill her coffee cup.

"But I don't know what that presence has to do with me," she continued as she poured half-and-half into her coffee mug and added the hot coffee over it.

"I do think I'm supposed to know about it, though, because the red moon is an omen of something bad coming. Why would I get an omen about something that had nothing to do with me, unless the universe can call a wrong number?"

She laughed at the thought of a large, bearded man consulting a list of people to dial up omens for.

Murphy started to whine for his breakfast. While he took his job as a Good Boy who kept his human safe seriously, breakfast was breakfast, and he was—after all—still a dog. As he wolfed down his kibble and canned pumpkin, Ashlynne buttered a bagel that popped up from the toaster filling the kitchen with the comforting smell of warm bread. With the morning sun shining in the front windows, cranked open to let the May breeze in, and the back garden's moonlit gloom retreating into the lake beyond, the ominous atmosphere of the night seemed far away.

Ashlynne let Murphy out into the dog run and returned to the kitchen to rinse the dishes and add them to the dishwasher. She suspected that she would run out of energy quickly since she had managed to miss half of her night's sleep. She thought it best she got some work done before sleepiness overtook her.

Checking to see that Murphy was OK and smiling to see him snoozing in a puddle of early morning sunlight, Ashlynne took the house manual to the settee in the sunroom and flipped through its pages until she found the section marked Guests. She spent the better part of the morning munching on her bagel and some fruit from the baskets on the table, reading, and acquainting herself with what was expected of her when guests were in attendance. She was relieved to see that it wasn't too different from waitressing—with some laundry thrown in for good measure.

She was expected to have coffee ready in the morning as well as an assortment of teas and pastries. Guests' beds were to be remade once they had vacated their bedrooms for the day and fresh bath linens put out. With seven guests in residence, this would more than likely keep her hopping for the better part of the mornings and early afternoons. During the evenings she would be expected to set out cheese and fruits to pair with the wines in the butler's pantry for guests to have before dinner. Then there were the twice-weekly housekeepers that she was required to manage, though that wasn't as big a deal as it originally sounded.

The housekeepers had serviced Rosehaven for many years and had their schedule down pat. On Mondays, they did the lower level and main floor. On Wednesdays, they did the second and third floors and the front and back porches. She noted that with a house this size, it takes a battalion of skilled workers to keep it going, and the housekeepers were just one aspect of that. Three times a week the gardeners arrived at dawn and were gone before nine o'clock to not disturb any guests who might want to have their morning coffee on the back porch.

Every Friday the florist brought baskets of fresh flowers and refreshed and replaced the over twenty floral arrangements that adorned various rooms throughout the house. Grocery orders would be placed every Sunday for delivery on Monday, and any catering needed throughout the week would be called in from any of the five approved caterers listed in the manual. All of this occurred with no cash or cards exchanged but with all services billed to the estate's accountant in September. All Ashlynne had to do was keep track of and maintain the already set schedule, carefully designed to run in the background and out of sight and knowledge of guests.

Having read and re-read what she would need to do, and feeling confident that she understood the procedures, she let Murphy in and went back to her rooms to shower and dress. The guests would be arriving in just a few more days, so the bathrooms needed to be prepared with fresh linens and the windows opened in each suite to allow the lake's breeze to freshen the stale air.

As she remade her bed and found clothes for the day, Ashlynne wondered again who the group was that she would be spending her summer with. What kind of business rented such a massive house for a whole summer and why?

Cranking the water to a temperature just north of hot, she stepped under the spray and felt the remainder of last night's weirdness sluice away and down the drain. Determined to make this summer lucrative as well as enjoyable, Ashlynne washed, toweled off, and pulled her clothes on to begin the day.

Chapter 10

The mid-afternoon sun shone brightly through the tall windows of Rosehaven, showcasing the brilliant spring sky beyond.

"C'mon, Murphy, let's go for a walk and look around this town before we're swamped with guests and work."

Ashlynne slipped her feet into tennis shoes and clipped Murphy's leash to his halter. She decided to grab a lightweight sweater, and sadness bloomed unexpectedly in her chest, vowing to contact Mimi this evening no matter what. She missed the smoke rings and snarky advice that came from the spirit more than she thought possible.

Grabbing her sunglasses and slipping the

house key into the pocket of her jeans, she let Murphy lead the way out the service door and down the cobbled driveway to the sidewalk. They turned right and ambled down the dappled cement path, the sun playing hide and seek through the leaves of the maples and oaks that lined the genteel neighborhood's street.

Retracing their steps from their first night in Charlevoix, Ashlynne and Murphy crossed the two-lane drawbridge that separated the north side of the town from the south. The choppy Pine River Channel flowed beneath the bridge, emptying into Round Lake to her left and the expanse of Lake Michigan to her right. At the centermost section of the bridge, she and Murphy stopped, Murphy with his nose up catching the scent of the water. Ashlynne held her phone at eye-level to take a picture of the bright red lighthouse that stood as a sentinel at the mouth of the channel marking refuge for ships coming into port and warning those leaving of the dangers of Lake Michigan. She attached the picture to a text addressed to Andrew, hit send, and continued across the bridge to the main shopping district of the little town.

Bridge Street doubles as US Highway 31, making traffic control an organizational nightmare during the busy summer months, but as they walked, the car and pedestrian traffic were slow and leisurely. Ashlynne and Murphy matched the comfortable pace, both physically and mentally. She felt her shoulders drop from up near her ears, and her tongue loosened from the roof of her mouth; she had not realized the amount of stress her body had been holding. As she let out a sigh, she noticed that Murphy had stopped straining against his leash, now calm enough to walk at a slower pace.

"You too, huh?" she asked the small terrier who walked contentedly along beside her. Gifted with his sloppy doggy-grin, tongue lolling from the side of his mouth, Ashlynne smiled down at him and was grateful anew for his continued presence in her world.

They spent the afternoon strolling among the small shops and galleries that were open. As it was still early in the summer season, several storefronts remained papered with 'SEE YOU IN THE SUMMER' signs splashed across their plate glass windows, but there were enough shops open to make an afternoon of their adventure. Ashlynne was pleasantly surprised that her dog was welcome in all but one shop, and they wandered happily in and out of gift shops both high-end and not. One shop had beautifully framed works of local art depicting the red lighthouse in its myriad of moods and seasons, as well as landscape and garden scenes and dramatic renditions of large ships on the waves of Lake Michigan. The staggeringly high price tags hinted at the pocketbooks of the summer visitors.

"If I worked all summer and then cashed out the last of Mimi's money, I could probably get this one, Murphy," whispered Ashlynne pointing at a minuscule painting measuring less than three inches square. The well-dressed woman at the counter shot her a withering look; Ashlynne wasn't sure whether it was because she was talking to her dog or if she had heard her remark.

Flashing her best waitress smile at the disapproving clerk, Ashlynne chirped, "Thanks so much! This is a lovely gallery!" and made a quick exit out to the sunny sidewalk.

Giggling after the exchange, Ashlynne wandered into a gift shop dedicated only to items that had a lake theme, signs that said things like 'Life Is Better At The Lake' and 'Lake Life'; paper cocktail napkins with images of the state in its iconic mitten shape with a red star marking Charlevoix's location, and artisan pottery glazed in muted blues and browns. Birch-branch chairs held throw pillows with images of Labradors and red pick-up trucks. Whitewashed shelving held wine glasses with dark green pine trees painted onto the stems, and large baskets held bags of potpourri with names like 'pine forest' and 'beach stone'. Curious as to what 'beach stone' would smell like, Ashlynne leaned down and took a small sniff.

"It's cinnamon, Murphy," she whispered to the dog who was snorting and huffing trying to undo the scent-overload from the store that invaded his sensitive nose.

As they walked further into the store, Ashlynne found herself at odds with the manufactured calmness of it all; the serene color schemes, the signs with their homey sayings, the perfectly placed platters holding cottage-aesthetic coasters and wine glasses. Everything felt vastly different from the raucous colors and textures found in the French Quarter's shops. This was pretty, to be sure, but seemed out of step with the world at large.

"Maybe that's the point, Murph," mused Ashlynne as they left the aggressively serene store.

"Maybe people who visit here want a version of life that insists on safety, serenity, and artistically displayed comfort. Life as a window-dressing. I don't get it, but when I lived up here the group homes didn't have decorative throw pillows, and if you were caught with a bowl of potpourri, you were probably going to be arrested, even if it was called Beach Stone," she chuckled ruefully.

They stopped to look in the window of a jewelry store but decided to not go in, lovely as the wares looked. Feelings of insecurity and shame crept up on her; holdovers from her time as a child here that she had been certain she had overcome—until now. The expensive art galleries, the militant perfection of the home goods shops, and the smooth disapproval of the clerks had all combined to send her careening emotionally back to her scared and lonely teenaged self.

They stopped as Murphy began slurping loudly from a red plastic bowl filled with water set outside of a small ice cream parlor. Ashlynne looked through the windows to see a pretty, welcoming space with gleaming white counters. The tiny dark-haired woman behind the cash register smiled in greeting, and Ashlynne returned the smile shyly. The thin, be-speckled gentleman standing behind the shopkeeper had passed away over fifty years ago but returned to the shop frequently, never having given up his dedication to its success. He noticed Ashlynne noticing him and smiled in surprise. She nodded gently in his direction and watched as he faded out of view.

"Want some ice cream, Murph?" she asked the dog who was busy finishing off the water in the bowl.

Opening the door a crack she called in, "Can my dog come inside?"

"Sure!" said the woman, her smile apparent in her voice. "I love dogs!" the woman said as Ashlynne approached the rounded, glass-fronted ice cream cooler.

"What kind is he?" the woman asked Ashlynne as she looked over the menu detailing ice cream flavors, fudge varieties, and caramel corn.

"He's a terrier mix, pretty much a mutt," replied Ashlynne, head swimming at the exciting selection of sugary wares.

"He's awfully cute and very well behaved," the woman complimented.

On cue, Murphy sat in his pretty position and favored the shopkeeper with his best doggy grin.

Laughing delightedly, the shopkeeper cried," Oh my! He is just the cutest thing ever!"

Ashlynne watched her dog mug

shamelessly and avoided rolling her eyes—but did reply with enough Mimi-inspired snark to catch Murphy's attention, "Oh yeah, he's cute, alright."

Catching the sarcastic tone in his human's voice, Murphy felt he may be overdoing his act and settled down onto the black and white checkered floor to wait for his ice cream.

Ashlynne decided on Mackinac Island Fudge for herself and plain vanilla for Murphy, along with a slice of chocolate fudge studded with black walnuts to take home. Ashlynne paid for her treats and led Murphy to the door.

"Thanks so much. This all looks wonderful!" she said to the shopkeeper.

"You're very welcome. We make everything in-house. The fudge is a family recipe that's been made the same way for close to one hundred years. My name is Cheri, what's yours?"

"I'm Ashlynne and this little guy is

Murphy," she replied, happy to have met a friendly person today.

"Hi, Ashlynne. Good to meet you. And hello to Murphy, too! Where are you from?" Cheri asked.

"Oh, kind of here and there," replied Ashlynne as nonchalantly as possible. Her honest personal history wasn't suitable for a casual meeting.

"I'm working for the summer at Rosehaven," Ashlynne continued.

"Oh! That house is gorgeous. I've always wanted to see the inside, lucky you!" exclaimed Cheri.

"It's awfully pretty," agreed Ashlynne, smiling at Cheri's enthusiasm.

"Well, you come back and say 'hi' anytime, Ashlynne! It's been great to meet a new face this early in the season," said Cheri, just as a young woman with a small tow-headed boy walked in.

"Thank you, Cheri. I will!" called

Ashlynne as she exited the small shop, letting the screen door slam shut behind her.

She sat down on the bench in front of the ice cream parlor and patted the space next to her. Murphy jumped up and sat down, careful to not overdo his enthusiasm so his human wouldn't withhold the beautiful bowl of vanilla ice cream.

"Here you go, ya' big ham," she said, and she set the small bowl down in front of him.

Ashlynne sat contentedly eating her ice cream and looking at the picture-perfect marina in front of her. She had made note of it when she and Murphy had arrived by bus, but it was night then, and their view wasn't nearly as beautiful as it was right now.

"This sure is a pretty little place, isn't it, Murphy?" she asked the dog who was busy slurping down every ounce of his ice cream.

Ashlynne sat across the street from East Park—its rolling green lawn currently dotted with a bandshell, fishponds, rock walls, and a flagpole flying a large American flag. As if looking at a double exposure photograph, Ashlynne could see weathered wooden buildings lining the water's edge and lengths of fishing nets strung on pylons to dry and be repaired wavering just behind the manicured park. Boardwalks, rather than cement sidewalks, ran the length of the street that was a mess of rutted mud and trampled hay. The town's earlier version of East Park was much more focused on logging and fishing than orchestras and yachts.

The grass in the modern-day park stopped at the marina which housed an amazing array of boats both palatial and modest. Round Lake reached out beyond the boat docks, flanked by Lake Charlevoix and the Pine River Channel that gave access to Lake Michigan.

Ashlynne observed the expanse of fresh water. The pretty drawbridge that they had walked across earlier opened and closed on schedule in the summer to allow larger crafts entry to either Lake Michigan or Round Lake depending on which direction they were moving. Right now, the bridge opened by demand as was evidenced by a tall-masted sailboat blowing its horn to signal its desire to enter Round Lake. The clanging of the bridge's bells responded to the boat's horn, and the safety gates dropped across both sides of the bridge, preventing road traffic from attempting to cross.

As each side of the bridge rose higher and higher, they eventually reached a height well over the town's tallest storefronts and buildings. It was impressive by any standard, and Ashlynne wasn't surprised in the least to see a small group of early-season tourists gathered at the safety gates taking photographs of the large boat as it made its way smoothly between the bridge's arms and into Round Lake to dock.

Gathering up the empty ice cream cups

and napkins and discarding them in one of the many trash cans lined up and down the street, she walked on, holding Murphy's leash in one hand and her bag of fudge in the other.

"When in Rome, Murph. When in Rome," she said to her dog who paid little attention to her and had no concept of her reference to Ambrose or human proverbs.

Ashlynne, however, marveled at not only being back in Northern Michigan but at being able to say that she was having enough of a touristy day to be labeled a Fudgy. While the word was often used by locals to mock tourists, as a child Ashlynne thought it was the most magical of things to be able to go on vacation and eat all the candy that you wanted.

Reaching the end of the shopping district, Ashlynne saw that she could cross the street to where a small grocery store was located that sported a logo she recognized; she was pleased to see in person where her weekly deliveries were coming from. The other options for their journey were to continue straight up Bridge Street and leave the downtown area, turn right onto Antrim Street and enter the more residential spaces, or cross the street and walk along the park side of the shopping district and back to the bridge. She opted for the last choice. The sun had peaked hours ago, and the wind was picking up. She noticed that several shops along the route she had walked along earlier were starting to close for the day and guessed that the rest would soon follow.

"They really close things up early here, don't they?" she asked the dog as they wandered past the bandshell and the park's lawn—with its shadows of taverns and rooming houses from the city's earliest days—and crossed the next corner to find another block of shops.

One gift shop caught her eye; it had a washed brick facade and iron balcony like the buildings in the French Quarter, but it was closed. Peering through the windows, she sighed wistfully. The interior showed imperfectly faded chintzes and linens, wonky-shaped, hand-cut soaps, and geraniums potted in moss-covered terracotta pots.

"I think I would have liked this store," she said to Murphy, and they continued walking under the massive baskets of petunias hanging gracefully from the lamp posts spaced evenly along the route. As they passed a yacht brokerage and a stand-up paddleboard dealer, she made a mental note to try and visit the pretty French shop sometime before she left for New Orleans.

Michigan Avenue was quiet and dim as they made their way back through the overhang of the hardwood's branches and turned up the cobbled driveway of Rosehaven. Ashlynne saw that several lights were burning on the uppermost floor and wondered if they were on timers or if perhaps

Eliza had lit them.

"We're home, Murph. Only we would be staying in a place where it's a toss-up as to whether the lamps are on timers, or the ghosts turn them on for us!" she laughed.

She unlocked the door and followed the dog into the service vestibule and into the kitchen beyond to decide what to eat for dinner.

Chapter 11

Ashlynne and Murphy enjoyed an easy dinner—sauteed vegetables and pasta with Parmesan cheese and cracked black pepper for Ashlynne and kibble with chopped zucchini for Murphy. In his usual form, Murphy gulped his dinner down as fast as possible so he had time to beg for bites of Ashlynne's food before she could finish.

"Uh-huh—not happening. Mine has lovely things like pepper and onions and garlic in it; none of which you can have, so just back off," she sternly told him through a mouthful of her dinner.

Murphy shot her a look of betrayal and wandered off into the front of the house, the spirits of the two white dogs trailing after him. Smiling to herself at the almost-human interactions from the terrier, Ashlynne decided to sample one of the white wines housed in the butler's pantry. After selecting the wine from a wide variety of bottles in the cooler, she pulled the cork with a satisfying pop and poured the yellow-gold liquid into a crystal stemmed wine glass.

"A girl could get used to all of this fanciness," she said as she returned to the kitchen to finish her solitary dinner.

As the sun finished its descent below the lake's horizon at the back of the house, veiling the front of the room in darkness, Ashlynne gathered her dishes to rinse and put into the dishwasher. She wiped down the counters and brushed off the butcher block tabletop, putting the kitchen to rights again.

"Murphy! Murph—come!" she called into the darkened expanse of the rooms beyond the kitchen's glow.

She noticed that small lamps were lit here and there within the music room and living room and made a mental note to find out if they were, in fact, on timers. Ashlynne carried her glass, the partially consumed bottle of wine, and her phone and went in search of the dog. After wandering the main floor with her wine glass in one hand and the bottle in the other, feeling a bit like a minor character in a Gothic novel, she finally located the dog as he was nosing around in the library. The dark red walls and the hand-painted map on the ceiling cemented the Gothic atmosphere of the evening and made Ashlynne wonder if the homeowner had spent any significant amount of time in England.

Shooing Murphy out from under the heavy mahogany desk and following him out into the foyer, Ashlynne decided to take the main staircase up to the second floor—its grand, sweeping arch fit with the strange ambiance of the evening.

"I just need a taffeta gown falling fetchingly off of one shoulder with my hair piled on top of my head," she said to the dog who continued to ignore her.

As she took the first step onto the stairs, the hairs on the back of her neck stood painfully and goosebumps ran unchecked up and down her arms. A heaviness, more akin to pressure than to pain, settled in her lower abdomen.

Setting the wine glass and bottle down very carefully, Ashlynne gripped the railing and closed her eyes. She was unsure whether the wine or the dinner caused this sudden feeling of upset. She sat down on the step, letting her eyes fall closed again.

Images exploded behind her eyelids: a large owl flying over the house, a woman standing with her arm outstretched as an enormous wolf approached her, a small natural spring surrounded by ancient cedar trees, and the moon-ringed in a haze of brilliant red. The pressure in her gut and the goosebumps running rampant up and down her arms continued unabated as she tried to make sense of the images, but they didn't seem to have anything in common with each other. She opened her eyes and found herself directly in line with the music room, looking at its ornate baby grand piano, antique lap harps, and fringed ottoman that held an array of books and loose sheet music. Standing on a small table next to the piano was a large doll. It was ornately clad in a Victorian petticoat and dress, its dark brown hair arranged atop its head with a feathered hat perched on top. The doll's features were strangely waxen, though Ashlynne thought it must have a porcelain face. The doll's eyes were brilliant and lively. Normally, Ashlynne would be impressed with the creator's skill in crafting something so at odds with itself—textured skin on smooth porcelain and eyes that had

genuine depth yet were obviously painted—
but the current effect was seductively sinister.
How had she never noticed this doll?
Granted, she tended to use the back stairway
and rarely came this far into the front rooms
of the house, but surely she would have seen
this doll before now, if only because it was so
creepy.

"Maybe it's not as scary in the daylight?"
she asked Murphy who had sat down beside
her.

Murphy looked over at his mistress when
her voice broke, leaning more of his small
body against hers.

Ashlynne took a sip of her wine and gazed
at the doll, wondering why it affected her so
badly and if this had anything to do with the
images that she had seen. She mentally
flipped through the scenes. She first
remembered the owl then the wolf—bigger
than anything she had ever seen on a nature
documentary, but she had never seen a wolf

in real life, so she had no idea if the one from her vision was unnaturally large or not. Then the memory of the woman who held the wolf off, but she didn't look familiar and certainly didn't share a likeness with the doll. The image of the moon was the same one that had woke her, and its ominous warning still seemed to hold, but what danger was approaching and from where?

The hard wooden steps were growing cold, and Ashlynne no longer wanted to stay there. She was afraid to turn her back to the doll but walking backward up the staircase presented its own dangers. Unable to make a decision, she continued to sip her wine and stare at the ornately dressed figurine, almost daring it to do something—anything.

After twenty minutes, the doll had not moved, but Ashlynne's butt felt numb from sitting, and she decided that she would simply have to make a move. She couldn't sit on the steps all night. Taking a deep breath,

she stood with as much courage as she could
muster and stepped purposefully down the
last two steps, scurrying quickly past the
music room and into the small service
vestibule to her left. Flicking on every light
within reach, she ran up the service staircase
and came to a panting halt at the landing on
the second floor. Only pausing for a moment,
she then hurried past the last several feet to
her door, and she could hear the lights click
off along the staircase behind her.

Thoroughly spooked, she pushed open her
door, shoved Murphy in with her foot, and
slammed it closed behind them.

She paused to catch her breath, poured
wine to the rim of her glass, took a long
swallow, and wiped her mouth with the back
of her hand.

"Well, there's one mystery solved, Murph.
No timers on the lights!"

It took her a minute to realize that the
hysterical laughter she heard was her own,

and she covered her mouth like a five-year-old who had just said her first curse word.

Taking a halting breath, Ashlynne walked down the small hall in her suite and into the sitting room that she rarely used. While the room was pretty, her bedroom had access to the balcony, so she spent most of her time there. The sitting room, however, had an ornate full-length mirror, exactly what she needed right now.

Dropping cross-legged in front of the mirror and sipping her wine, Ashlynne waited. Minutes ticked by from the tall casement clock behind her, but the glass only reflected her own image and the room in which she sat.

Beyond feeling silly at this point, Ashlynne called firmly," Mimi! Are you there? I need to talk to you!"

The clock tick-tocked some more, and the mirror showed nothing but her own reflection.

She stood and placed the wine bottle and glass on the table next to the mirror. She stood with her hands on her hips, unsure if she was feeling annoyed, or scared, or lonesome.

"I guess, all of those," she whispered as she walked out of the room.

"All of those what, Dear?" spoke the familiar, raspy voice from behind her.

"OH! Mimi! It's you! You're really here!" cried Ashlynne, running back into the sitting room.

"Of course, it's me, Dear. Who else would you be talking to in your mirror?"

"In this house? It's hard to tell!" she cried.

"Well, it is me for now. What's wrong? And why are you drinking?"

"I'm not drinking—I just had some wine with my dinner," replied Ashlynne, trying to keep the defensive tone from her voice.

"It looks like you've had an entire bottle of wine," replied Mimi, not at all trying to hide her judgment.

"Can we not do this? I've really missed you, and this house is a hot mess of crazy ghosts. There's a creepy doll downstairs next to the piano, and I have guests coming soon, and I don't know what to do!" Ashlynne finished in a wail as she crumpled cross-legged onto the floor in front of the mirror.

"Oh, my. Well, OK," stammered the spirit, surprised to see the young woman in a heap in front of her.

Mimi pulled a chair into view from the left of the mirror's frame, sat comfortably, and lit a cigarette—the irony in her previous judgment of Ashlynne's wine was lost on her.

"Ashlynne, look at me," demanded Mimi in between exhaling smoke rings above her head.

Ashlynne looked up from behind a curtain of red hair that fell over her face like a screen.

Mimi continued, "I'm sorry to have upset you, and I'm sorry you're not happy with this job so far, but remember when I said it would be perfect for someone with your skills?"

"Yeah," mumbled Ashlynne in the general direction of the mirror's glass.

"I hope you didn't think that I meant your skills as a waitress."

Ashlynne brushed the hair away from her face at Mimi's remark and looked directly at the spirit.

"What did you mean, exactly?" she asked coldly.

Unperturbed by her friend's tone, Mimi continued, "Surely someone with your skills and talents wasn't brought to a house like this one by mistake."

"My skills and talents," parroted Ashlynne in a tone that would have caused most people to step back to avoid the frigidness pouring out with every word.

"Stop it, Ashlynne. If you would quit pouting for one minute, you would be able to think more clearly. Please take a deep breath, settle yourself, and let's talk. There isn't much more time left before things get truly crazy in this house, and you need to be prepared," warned Mimi.

And Ashlynne obeyed. She gathered her strength, curbed her pride, and settled in to talk with her friend. The sun rose outside the windows of the sitting room as they concluded their reunion.

As Ashlynne stumbled into her bedroom, she felt calmer and more herself than she had since she and Murphy had boarded the bus that brought them to the beautiful town where this strangely alive house sat high above the waters of Lake Michigan. Forewarned, and therefore forearmed, Ashlynne fell headlong into a dreamless sleep ahead of the coming guests and the storm that they would bring.

Chapter 12

Mimi spent most of her time in the In-Between, the misty gap that separated the world of the living from the Light that gathered the dead back into itself. It was a soft and mutable place where other spirits floated past, lost in the memories of their most recent lives or, like Mimi, choosing to stay to interact just a little while longer with the living. Mimi hadn't planned on becoming part of Ashlynne's life. She had set up a nice little space for herself with her comfortable armchair and a never-ending supply of cigarettes, floating peacefully through the lavender mists and watching vignettes of human activity through various portals and mirrors. She moved along whenever her interest waned. Some humans retained more of the Light than others, and those humans shone brightly as spotlights through the purple mists; Ashlynne was one of those humans. In fact, Ashlynne shone brighter than any human Mimi had ever encountered.

The young woman's Light was breathtaking, and Mimi was intrigued. Even more intriguing was how Ashlynne could see spirits such as Mimi, a rare occurrence. And though she showed remarkable talent in other-worldly interaction, Ashlynne was still very young—a fact that was underscored during times such as this when the otherwise highly intuitive redhead seemed decidedly blind to the drama that was rapidly unfolding around her. Even more, Ashlynne seemed oblivious to the role she'd need to play to ensure a positive outcome.

Mimi stood and walked through the mists searching for the portal that would show her what she needed to know. As the wisps of the In-Between floated past, tickling her face and neck, she saw the dark red glow of the portal's opening. Dropping her cigarette and stubbing it out on the non-existent floor—an artifice that brought her comfort—she walked softly toward the ruby glow. The In-Between was a place without measurable time and tangible space. Everything and nothing existed here. For spirits who felt apprehensive about how to navigate the mists, it could feel both terrifying and lonely; most naturally found their way home to the Light in short order. For others, like Mimi, its nothingness provided abundant opportunities and potential.

The red energy bleeding out from the portal throbbed and pulsed, flecked through with sparks of dull metallic silver. Mimi stepped carefully to the side and peered through the angry crimson opening.

The woman who the owl called the Other

stood in front of a closet filled with clothes, an open suitcase on the bed behind her. She was small and dark, the ringlets of her hair framing her narrow face. The energy that radiated out from her was almost as blinding as Ashlynne's, though its angry crimson and dull silver hue had a darker tint than Ashlynne's candle-bright shine.

Mimi watched as Stella, the Other's true name, chose an assortment of clothing that she layered piece by piece into the waiting suitcase. Blouses were followed by slacks, and slacks were followed by t-shirts that were covered by shorts until the suitcase was filled to the brim.

The mundane nature of Stella's packing did not interest Mimi in the least. Carefully leaning further into the scene, Mimi was able to find what she was looking for; the Journey Stone sat amongst bottles of perfume and makeup scattered across the top of Stella's vanity. Mimi's face darkened in anger. For this woman to leave such an important item amongst bottles of perfume and wrinkle cream was hubris to a degree that was inconceivable. In Mimi's eyes, the stone glowed a warm chocolate brown with shimmers of green and gold. Its beauty was hidden from most human sight, though Stella Burnes knew exactly what it was and had wielded its immense power with a skill that still amazed Mimi given the current lackadaisical way it was stored.

"So many pieces to this puzzle had to be fitted with exact precision to undo the mess that was made, and you toss the stone on your dressing table next to your night cream like some dime store bauble?" complained Mimi under her breath.

The woman continued to pack, unaware of the spirit watching her through the framed mirror across the room.

Mimi moved away from the scene—a scene that had, in fact, occurred several days before, and was technically in Ashlynne's past. Mimi saw what she needed, though— the woman, Stella, had the stone and would bring it to Rosehaven. The Journey Stone: the magical rock that had the power to move spirits into and out of objects, whether they were inside of a human body or the representation of one.

Settling back into her overstuffed armchair and lighting her cigarette, Mimi called to the owl and watched as the enormous bird glided toward her from deep within the shifting purple mists. The owl perched on the back of her chair, watching smoke rings float one after the other only to disappear into the wispy air. Mimi crooned softly to the creature in response to the images it sent silently to her; the Witches would visit Ashlynne on this day in her world. Mimi watched as the owl sent images of the next days and weeks— disjointed pictures of Ashlynne running in terror, locked doors, and madly flickering lights within an enormous house. She saw impressions of Ashlynne wandering the misty In-Between, lost and scared, and a shattered doll staring out into nothingness. Finally, she saw the last image, an egg-shaped stone banded in white quartz and glowing a warm chocolate brown as it sank below the waves into the fathomless depths of Lake Michigan.

"Stop! Those are only whispers of what could be! Shadow-plays of an end result that could happen but needn't. It is why you called me, and it is why I'm here," hissed Mimi over her shoulder at the yellow-eyed bird perched behind her.

She waved her arm in an abrupt dismissal, "You've asked me to come and to bring Ashlynne, and I've asked you for a favor as well; go do that so that we can figure this mess out."

Mimi passed a scrap of paper back over her shoulder and felt the sharp beak take it from her hand. The owl took flight and banked sharply.

"No one likes a show-off," she called after the massive bird as it flew into the forever twilight of the mists.

In another time, just recently passed, the owl glided silent and unseen through the open window of a small shop in the magical city of New Orleans and slipped the ripped piece of paper which held the key to another mystery into a small blue book titled Faerie Tales.

Chapter 13

The coffee maker burbled and gurgled, releasing its aromatic brew as Ashlynne prepared Murphy's breakfast. The early morning sky outside the floor-to-ceiling windows at the back of the large kitchen and sunroom showed a gathering front of angry dark clouds on the lake's horizon. The windows in front of her, cranked open to allow the lake-scented breeze in, showed the tall maples and oaks that lined Michigan Avenue swaying in the gray morning air. The air was humid, heavy, and damp and Ashlynne felt homesick for New Orleans.

"I forgot how intense the storms on the lake can be," she said to the dog as she set his bowl in front of him.

The air felt alive with electricity. There was a crackling of energy that made the small hairs on her arms and the back of her neck stand up. It left her feeling antsy—maybe a brisk walk or even a jog would help to burn some of the pent-up power that settled within her body.

"I feel like a human lightning rod," muttered Ashlynne as she prepared her coffee and walked to the large windows in the sunroom.

Murphy, finished with his breakfast danced, and whined at her feet, ready to be let out into the dog run. Lost in her thoughts and wondering what should be done, Ashlynne stared out at the storm clouds piling one atop the other as they moved in over the expansive black waters of the lively lake. There were rumblings of faraway thunder, heralding the storm to come.

Wondering why Ashlynne ignored him,

Murphy finally let out a series of yips to alert his mistress that now was a very good time to let him outside. His efforts were rewarded when the French door pushed open, allowing him to skitter out onto the massive flagstones and around the corner to his dog-run. Ashlynne barely unlatched the small gate when he pushed his way through, making haste to his favored patch of grass in the corner.

Hardly any of these events registered with Ashlynne who was still planning her day. She went back into the artificially lit sunroom and climbed up the steps to the kitchen to refill her coffee. She heard footfalls from deep within the house, pacing-pacing-pacing -up the stairs, across the floor above her, down the stairs, through the main floor rooms, back up the stairs—a seemingly endless loop fraught with anxiety and fear. Ashlynne felt Eliza's emotions wash through the house, and she wondered if the energy from the oncoming storm set the spirit into this state or if she also knew of—or could feel the presence of—the group that would arrive soon. Ashlynne reached out to calm her only to be met with worry and distress; a tangled ball of blue energy, jumping and whizzing, bounced off the walls and ceilings.

"I know just how you feel. I'll do my best to make sure this all turns out OK, I promise," Ashlynne whispered to the spirit.

Lights throughout the massive house flickered off and on in response. Ashlynne, resolved to follow through on her vow, carried her coffee outside to gather her thoughts and prepare for the Witches' arrival.

The sun never seemed to rise, and though the sky did brighten at dawn, it only made the storm clouds appear darker. Ashlynne sat on the back porch, listening to the lake, and catching glimpses of Eliza who watered the potted plants and ferns throughout the expansive garden. The spirit's image flickered into and out of view like an old-fashioned television screen that couldn't find a strong broadcast. Ashlynne assumed the flickering was caused by either the erratic energy from the coming storm or by Eliza's anxiety.

"Maybe everything is tense today," she whispered to Murphy who sat as close to her as possible without climbing into her lap.

"We're all feeling it, aren't we?" she asked her small companion, ruffling the fur on the top of his ears.

"But whatever—or whoever—we're feeling is getting closer, so we need to get to work. I'm going to get dressed and then we're going for a walk, Murphy."

Murphy eyed the darkening sky and thought a walk was probably not the best idea but knew he didn't get a vote in the day's activities. Heaving a sigh full of trepidation, he shuffled down the steps and followed Ashlynne through the tall French doors back into the sunroom. They left Eliza to flicker in and out sporadically as she continued to water and re-water the ferns and geraniums in a continual loop of anxious worry.

Ashlynne rinsed her coffee cup and Murphy's breakfast bowl then went up the back steps to the second floor. The house was darker here, away from the kitchen with its expanse of windows and lit chandeliers.

The small lamp perched on the dainty table outside her rooms was lit, casting a warm glow onto the damask-papered walls. The light puddled onto the dark hardwood floors, and Ashlynne smiled. Sending out a subtle thank you to Eliza, she pushed open the heavy wooden door and entered her suite. Nearly as dark as the stairwell, with no welcoming lamps lit, Ashlynne studied the space with new eyes. Where in the small suite would be the best hiding place?

She pulled on a pair of shorts and stuck her feet into running shoes. There was a problem pressing against her mind; her bedroom wasn't suitable. She needed the ability to sleep without the additional creepy atmosphere that this situation brought. The sitting room could work, but she identified the space as her meeting room for conversations with Mimi and didn't want to be overheard if that was a possibility. Braiding her hair down her back she continued her planning. Certainly not the bathroom—the thought of being not only seen but heard as she was undressed or otherwise indisposed was enough to make her physically cringe, so that left the large walk-in closet in the hall between the bathroom and the sitting room.

Ashlynne had chosen not to utilize the large closet. She had few belongings that needed to be hung up and preferred to store her personal clothing within the same room where she slept. Ultimately, she wasn't familiar with the space. After turning the cold water tap off, she placed her toothbrush into the holder and took a deep breath.

"Well, Murphy, let's take a look at this closet, shall we?" she prompted.

Together, they walked down the short hallway and opened the door just before the 'T' at the end of the hallway and directed them either left to the bedroom or right to the sitting room. Turning the cut-glass doorknob, Ashlynne pushed the door open and clicked on the overhead light. The closet was easily as large as a small bedroom in a New Orleans apartment and outfitted with rods for hanging clothing, cedar-lined cubicles for sweaters, smaller squares for individual pairs of shoes, shelves for handbags, and two sets of narrow bookshelves with drawers below them that flanked the door, right and left.

Ashlynne knew the purpose of each cubby, shelf, and drawer because the closet was far from empty. In fact, it was crammed full of bags, shoes, sweaters, and pants. On one side hung nothing but elaborate ball gowns fit for a night at the opera or theater, and Ashlynne wondered where the owner had traveled to attend such an event, considering how Northern Michigan was much more laid back and casual than full-length silk gloves and heavy velvet gowns.

The bookshelves were stuffed full of all categories of books from drugstore paperbacks to heavy, leather-encased encyclopedias on gardening and history. The drawers beneath held a dizzying array of necklaces, rings, earrings, and pins—some looking quite expensive, others nothing more than dime-store finds—as well as trinkets and keepsakes such as wine corks, receipts, notes scrawled on scraps of tissue, and assorted pebbles, feathers, and dried flowers.

"Wow," whispered Ashlynne as Murphy let out a muffled sneeze from deep within the closet's recesses.

"I guess this will do just fine as a hiding place," she decided.

Pushing aside a velvet gown, she nudged the curious canine with one toe, scooting him toward the door.

"OK, Murph. One item on the to-do list is done. We found a hiding spot. Let's finish the rest of the list before the sky opens up on us, shall we?" she encouraged.

After returning to her suite, she closed the doors to her balcony, fighting against the storm that moved in across the lake. Turning her bedside lamp on for good measure, Ashlynne and Murphy closed the door to their suite and hurried down the stairs to the dark service vestibule, heading toward the lamp-lit kitchen and sunroom.

She ripped a piece of paper from the notebook on the kitchen table and stuffed it into the pocket of her shorts; she would need the information scrawled below the list and didn't trust herself to remember everything without it.

She pushed the door to the back garden

open and hit the heavy air, still and quiet as the storm gathered force and moved steadily inland. Taking a deep breath, she steadied herself against the oppressive atmosphere and her mounting anxiety and headed toward the steps that led down the cliff face to the beach below.

Chapter 14

The wind had whipped the lake into a fury with waves cresting over five feet at the shoreline by the time Ashlynne and Murphy made it down the steps to the beach below Rosehaven.

"I don't think I've ever seen a lake with waves like this!" yelled Ashlynne to the dog.

Murphy heard nothing but the crash of water on stones and sand as the wind grabbed his human's voice and tossed it down the beach toward the Pine River Channel and the bright red lighthouse beyond.

"OK, we need three unakite stones, two jasper stones—one yellow and one red—and one large Petoskey stone the size of an egg," muttered Ashlynne as she tried desperately to hold on to the scrap of paper that held her written notes.

"Thank God for the Internet," she continued. "Aside from the Petoskey stone, I've never heard of the others, let alone know what they look like!" she shouted, her voice barely audible over the roar of the lake.

Stuffing her notes back into her pocket and retrieving her phone, she searched for images of the stones that Mimi had instructed her to collect.

"Huh, unakite is really pretty," she said to Murphy, showing him the image on the phone. It occurred to her that this action might indicate that she needed more human friends, and she felt her cheeks flush in embarrassment.

"Anyway, let's see if we can find three of these babies, shall we?"

Walking as close to the waterline as possible without being drenched by the storm-driven waves, Ashlynne and Murphy assumed the timeless stance of beachcombers worldwide—heads down, eyes scanning the space in front of them as they shuffled along looking for the unique stone that would provide its energies and powers to the magic she would need very shortly.

"Ah-ha! Here's one!" cried Ashlynne in triumph as she snatched up the green and yellow stone before one of the lake's huge waves could carry it back out of reach. Murphy, though appearing to be looking for stones, kept his nose-down position and was not at all interested in the stones and rocks that his mistress sought. He was, in fact, so caught up in the amazing smells that he hardly knew she stopped to drop the stone into the grocery bag that she had brought along until his leash tightened and drew him up short.

"One down, a half dozen or so to go," said Ashlynne into the wind as she continued her slow walk down the beach.

During her search, she found two more unakites, one large red jasper and two yellow jaspers. While she had gathered four tiny, pebble-sized Petoskey Stones, she had yet to locate one in the size that Mimi had described.

Ashlynne noticed that Murphy was beginning to lose interest in the beach smells, and she was beginning to shiver from the unrelenting wind that continued to buffet her as it rushed in over the 55-degree waters of Lake Michigan.

"Let's finish up down here and move into the trees away from the lake, Murphy."

Ashlynne removed two empty and clean wine bottles from her supplies and filled one with sand and one with lake water. She secured each bottle with their own corks and wished she had brought a towel to dry off. She stowed the bottles back in the bag and climbed the gentle slope of sand that led them back into the copse of cedar trees above the beach. The sudden cessation of wind left her ears ringing and caused her dog to sit down suddenly on the soft loam. His continued attempts to stay upright in the beach's windstorm had left him limp with exhaustion.

Leaving Murphy to rest out of the gale, Ashlynne dropped the leash and consulted her notes, "Cedar—just cedar? No specific amount or part of the tree? Just cedar, ugh! Why didn't I write down better notes?"

She decided to make do with the information she could remember and carefully twisted small branches from the larger tree making sure to take those with the most greenery. With a nod to her friend Michele, a talented and devout Voodoo Priestess, and with no idea about the correct etiquette for this type of thing, Ashlynne placed three bright pennies at the base of the ancient tree and whispered a thank you for its provisions toward her upcoming work.

"Murphy, should we have left something

on the beach for the lake?" she asked and looked over her shoulder to see the dog fast asleep, covered in cedar needles and beach sand.

"I think I should," she answered herself and quickly ran back down to the water's edge where she fished out the last of the change in her pocket—a quarter, two nickels, and a dime. Laying them in the sand and stepping back she sent out a heartfelt thank you as she watched the next wave scoop up the offering and whisk it back out into the dark, roiling waters of the lake.

She returned to the shelter of the cedar trees and found Murphy still asleep. She looped the leash and the handle of the grocery bag over her wrist then hoisted her dog up, resting him on one hip. Murphy opened one eye, blinked slowly, then rested his head on her shoulder—his soft snuffles and snores indicated both exhaustion and deep contentment.

Ashlynne's own huffing and puffing after the thirty-fifth step on the steep cliff face certainly indicated exhaustion but was sorely lacking in contentment. By step forty-five, she decided that Murphy had rested enough. She set him down on the landing as she gasped for air and mentally chastised herself for not getting enough regular exercise. By the last step, number sixty-five, she dragged a ragged breath into her burning lungs and vowed to take better care of herself from now on.

The wind felt brisk away from the beach but didn't have the gale force that was playing out on the water's edge. As Ashlynne and Murphy made their way through the garden to the back door of Rosehaven's sunroom, the dog slowed his pace and a low, threatening growl emitted from the back of his throat. At the same moment, Ashlynne stopped dead in her tracks as the massive owl came to light on the flagstones a few feet from them, effectively blocking their way to the door.

Murphy continued his menacing growl but moved no further. Ashlynne watched as the enormous bird lifted one clawed talon and dropped a large object onto the pathway where it clattered and rolled toward them. Fixing them with a look both lively and cold, the bird of prey bobbed its head at the item to ensure that the young woman and dog both noticed. The owl launched itself into the sky with its powerful wings, slicing through the strong wind as if it were a gentle breeze.

As the enormous bird took flight, Ashlynne ducked reflexively and watched as its muscular wings powered it through the gusty winds and over the lake beyond.

"It's gone, Murph," she said to the small but mighty warrior at her feet, reaching down to ruffle his forehead.

Murphy's growl subsided to an occasional grumble that seemed more offended by the intrusion than alarmed or afraid.

Ashlynne led Murphy forward to the object that the owl had dropped. She peered at it quizzically. Murphy nosed at it carefully, noting that it only smelled of the beach with a tiny whiff of evergreen. The owl, itself, seemed to not have any scent, something he continued to find disturbing.

"What the hell?" whispered Ashlynne as she bent down to pick up the stone.

Measuring about two inches long, the nondescript gray stone was roughly oblong in shape and felt smooth. It was utterly unremarkable.

Murphy pressed his nose into the gray rock trying to find any trace of scent from the bird that had brought it. So intent was he in his quest that his human's shriek sent him scuttling backward in surprise.

"Hey! Look! Look, Murphy!" yelled Ashlynne as she snatched up the rock and held it out in front of her. It's a Petoskey stone! And it's big, too—easily the size of an egg!"

At the location where Murphy's cold, wet nose had connected with the stone, the telltale hexagon and eye pattern of the three hundred fifty-million-year-old fossil was visible.

"Where do you think the owl came from?" she asked Murphy as she placed the last stone they needed into the bag and led the dog into the back door of the house.

"I've seen the owl before. It's been in my dreams, but it doesn't seem to have any real feeling to it, you know?" she chattered as she laid her beach finds out on the butcher block top of the enormous kitchen table.

Ashlynne unclipped Murphy from his harness and leash and watched as he hopped onto one of the overstuffed settees in the sunroom and promptly fell asleep. She felt strangely hurt by Murphy's dismissal and reminded herself to find some humans to talk to soon. She threw away the sandy bag and washed the stones off in the deep porcelain sink.

As the water washed over them, their unique colors and patterns emerged, and Ashlynne smiled at the beauty of each one. The unakite stones featured spring-green bands, dotted with patches of peachy-pink and yellow. The jaspers, both yellow and red, were incredibly dense and opaque—their colors consistent having no other bands or patches. The Petoskey stones were simply fascinating, no matter their size; from one the size of her thumbnail to the large one dropped by the owl, their hexagon patterns and dark centers in each eye were consistent throughout. They were hypnotic. The colors ranged from dark grays and blacks to a few with dark greens and a subtle pink hue.

Ashlynne placed a plain white bar towel on the table and set the stones, cedar branches, and bottles holding the sand and water onto it. She looked over her supplies.

"Protection, Grounding, Cleansing,

Power, Banishing, and Purification. Let's hope this works," she whispered into the depths of the house and was not surprised to hear the chiming of a bell from within the darkened rooms.

Chapter 15

Ashlynne awoke in the dark shadow of an early morning storm unlike anything she had ever experienced; winds lashed the lakeside of Rosehaven, grabbing the exterior shutters and slamming them back into the clapboard siding with enough force to rattle the windows in their frames. The trees ringing the knot garden were bent almost in half as the gale-force winds rocketed in from the black roiling waters of the angry lake below the cliff.

As she pulled the duvet back up over the down comforter and piled the decorative pillows into place at the bed's ornate headboard, lightning flashed a kaleidoscope spectrum of brilliance about the bedroom.

Thunder crashed in response to the spectacular light show.

"Murphy, let's go!" called Ashlynne to the dog who was trying his hardest to burrow back under the covers; the combination of the violent storm and the early hour left him little enthusiasm for anything other than the warmth of the bed and a few more hours of sleep.

"I said move it," encouraged his mistress firmly as she physically placed him into the hall between their bedroom and the sitting room beyond.

Ashlynne caught him eying the door as a potential sanctuary, and she quickly closed the bedroom door then the sitting room door, leaving him no passage except the bathroom or the option to wait by the door of their suite that led to the second-floor landing. Feeling grumpy and out of sorts, Murphy sat by the door, head hung low and eyes droopy.

So caught up in the tasks that she still

needed to finish before the group—Dark Grove— arrived, the uncharacteristic temper tantrum from her dog went completely unnoticed by Ashlynne. She splashed water on her face, applied a quick swipe of moisturizer, brushed her teeth, and yanked her hair back into a messy ponytail. Striding quickly past the pouting canine, she opened the door to the bedroom, stripped off her sweats, and pulled on a pair of jeans and a long-sleeved t-shirt against the chill of the storm. As she was looking for her sneakers, Murphy slipped back into the suite, unseen, and scooted under the bed. Perfectly content to stay right there, he closed his eyes as he heard Ashlynne's footfalls exit the room and the heavy wooden door close against the hall's overhead light.

Ashlynne stepped quickly down the service stairs and turned into the butler's pantry to the kitchen. Wishing for the thousandth time since she had arrived that the coffee maker was on a timer like hers back home, she yawned deeply, spooned the fragrant grounds into the filtered basket, and poured in the water.

She consulted her notes and the supplies on the table, putting a check next to what she had either collected or accomplished. The few tasks left were completely doable before the group arrived at four o'clock.

She didn't notice Murphy underfoot and suspected, rightly so, that he had found a way to stay in bed. Ashlynne poured her coffee and put her breakfast into the toaster. As she waited for her bagel, she entered the formal dining room in search of candles. She needed four in total—one red, one blue, one yellow, and one either brown or black according to Mimi. She discovered the buffets and breakfronts were all locked and heard her bagel pop up from the kitchen. Breakfast and coffee were consumed before she would try to locate the key to the dining room cabinets. It was, after all, just now six in the morning, so she had time to eat and caffeinate before she fell too far into her worklist.

Ashlynne was just finishing her bagel and pouring a second cup of coffee when the rain began; it slashed and beat against the house, seeming to come from every direction. The rain's effect made the enormous structure feel much smaller as if the rainwater could move the walls inward by several feet. In a house this large it should have felt cozy. Instead, it felt stifling and strangely claustrophobic.

She picked through the myriad of keys in the small, zippered pouch provided to her with the house manual and located the skeleton key that could unlock various cabinets and buffets in the main floor's public rooms.

As the lightning sent strobing lights dancing off the walls, Ashlynne fitted the key first into an ornately carved breakfront whose top cabinet was filled with romantic figurines from Italy. The lower shelves held folded lace tablecloths between layers of delicate tissue and the accompanying drawers held napkin rings of leaded crystal, monogrammed napkins edged in the same lace as the tablecloths, as well as small cut glass place holders fitted with business card-sized stationary ready for a name to be inscribed.

Not finding any candles, she closed the drawers, cabinets, and glass-fronted doors and locked them all. Two more armoires provided more table lines, small bone dishes, and delicate salt cellars. One drawer held nothing but cocktail forks—forks for olives, forks for seafood, and forks for removing bones from meat.

While the contents of the cabinets were interesting, Ashlynne felt frustrated. With the hundreds of candlesticks scattered around the house, there had to be a cache of candles somewhere.

"Ah-ha! Finally!" she announced with

pleasure as a deep drawer within yet another carved cabinet proved to hold taper candles of all sizes, widths, and lengths. There were only a couple of colors—mostly greens, reds, creams, and a few yellows—but in the next drawer were boxes and boxes of votive candles in a veritable rainbow of hues. The candles were bright and golden yellow, berry-red, maroon, pine-needle green, and a delicate yellow-green that reminded Ashlynne of the ferns on the porches. Other candles were brilliantly white, and some were the color of old parchment. Finally, she noticed a box of beautiful violet and deep purple candles and at least eight shades of pink that she could grab without digging too far down into the drawer's recesses.

"Jackpot!" Ashlynne removed two of each color that she needed and decided that it would be best to take more than the list specified and have them rather than find out she needed more later. Whatever wasn't used she would return to the drawer.

Next on her list was blue thread. Having no idea where to find this item, she returned to the kitchen with the newly acquired candles for more coffee.

"Let's see, if I were a spool of blue thread, where in tens of thousands of square feet of this house might I be?" she asked into her coffee cup.

Taking a sip, she mentally wandered the various halls and rooms of Rosehaven and finally decided to start right there in the kitchen.

"Every kitchen has a junk drawer. It's almost a law," she said, scanning the perimeter of the large room.

There had to be at least thirty drawers in the space. Sighing heavily, she downed the last of her coffee and decided to search the sunroom side of the kitchen and work her way around until she either reached the refrigerator or a junk drawer—the latter happened first.

As there were no keys for the kitchen drawers, the search went faster than it did in the dining room, and the fabled junk drawer proved to be just before the refrigerator. Holding both hands heavenward and intoning a reverent "Aaaahhhhhh" in an unfortunate impersonation of a celestial choir, Ashlynne began pulling through the drawer and its odd assortment of stuff.

After sifting through staplers, far too many pens, paper clips, single birthday candles, wine corks, two plastic forks, an advertisement for a ski resort in Colorado, receipts from the local dry cleaners, a blue jay feather, three dried up glue sticks, and an unknown number of pennies, Ashlynne found a small plastic case holding the supplies necessary to replace a button or tack up a hem. She held her breath, hoping that there was blue thread inside of the sewing kit, and she popped open the lid and smiled. She found red, white, yellow, and blue mini spools of thread with a few coordinating buttons, a small needle, and a tiny seam ripper. She added the whole kit to her growing pile of supplies, poured another cup of coffee, and replaced the contents of the drawer. It closed with a satisfying clunk.

As the rain poured unabated and the wind howled as it raced in off the lake, Ashlynne checked the clock on the microwave.

"Six forty-five. Time to finish this up, I guess," she whispered to herself. The scavenger hunt for the last of her supplies had kept her mind occupied and free of the worry that had plagued her since her last chat with Mimi. Now, however, with just a few short hours to get the rest of her list completed before Dark Grove arrived, her anxiety returned in full force, and she could feel her heart tripping around behind her ribcage.

Ashlynne stood on tippy-toe and retrieved a wicker basket from a decorative shelf in the sunroom. Whisking away the delicate lace of spiders past, she carried it to the kitchen table and filled it with the supplies. Slipping the basket's handle over her arm, she went to the music room for the last item on her list.

The doll stood on its pedestal to the right of the baby grand piano, giving it a direct view of the front foyer and grand staircase. Now she understood why the doll was there and why it must be protected. Her new understanding didn't quell the creepiness of it, however. In fact, knowing the whole story made it even more frightening. A life-like doll is one thing. A doll filled with someone's life is quite another.

Peering into the doll's eyes, Ashlynne whispered, "Meredith? Are you in there?"

The complete lack of response felt more unnerving than whatever response she had imagined, making her move as quickly as possible without harming the figure.

She wrapped it carefully in the fringed silk shawl that was draped over the piano and, tucking the bundle securely under her arm above the basket's handle, ran quickly up the grand staircase.

Lightning flashed and sparked off the crystals that dripped from the enormous chandelier that hung suspended between the second and third floors in the stairwell as she rounded the graceful curve and stepped out onto the second-floor landing between her suite and the owner's suite to her right. As thunder rumbled and rolled across the roof of Rosehaven, Ashlynne and her basket of supplies, along with the enchanted doll wrapped in silk, entered her suite. She closed the door securely behind her—locking it for good measure.

Ashlynne checked her notes. Considering how many times she had checked them over the past few days, she thought she should have memorized them by now.

"Hide the doll—and hide it well—then set the wards," she read aloud.

At the sound of his mistress's voice, Murphy peaked his head out from under the bed and watched as Ashlynne gently picked up the doll wrapped in silk and carried it into the suite's hallway. Padding along after her, Murphy saw Ashlynne open the heavy wooden door of the closet and click the light on.

Moving aside the assorted ball gowns, velvet wraps, and furs, Ashlynne found the old suitcase she had stashed earlier. The size was perfect for the doll.

She set the bundle down carefully, pulled the golden-brown monogrammed case from behind the formal wear, and snapped its burnished brass clasp open with an audible click. Lifting the lid sent a cloud of mothball-scented dust into the closet, and Murphy sneezed loudly behind her.

"Well, look who's decided to join me. Did you go back to bed, you bum?" Ashlynne teased as her dog trotted into the closet to investigate.

Whining softly as he sniffed the bundle containing the doll and nosing it suspiciously, he leveled Ashlynne with a look that suggested, this is going to be big trouble!

She ignored his look and its message and placed the doll into the mini trunk, tightly closing the lid. She hefted the trunk back into place behind the clothing and rearranged the gowns and furs so that everything hung straight.

"OK, onto the next part of this. I'm not sure what I'm more afraid of right now, Murph—an enchanted doll in my closet, having to perform magic I don't know much about without Michele or Andrew here, or the group coming that will try to break through it."

Aside from a quick break to let Murphy outside and give him his breakfast, Ashlynne spent the rest of the morning setting up the magical wards and barriers that would, hopefully, keep Meredith safe while she was imprisoned within the doll.

Using the compass app on her phone, she located the correct directional points within her suite and placed the corresponding candles at each direction; blue in the west at the French Doors in her bedroom, red at the windows in her bathroom that faced south, yellow on the small table in front of the windows that faced east in her sitting room, and the brown candle on a hamper that she moved from her bedroom to the left of the door of her suite that led to the landing, to the north. Each candle was then set into a glass dish that was filled with a small amount of sand from the beach.

Next, she gathered most of the cedar branches into a bundle, wound tightly with the blue thread. After that, she moved to the stones. Unakite, used for balancing the physical and the spiritual, she set one on top of the small trunk in her closet that hid the doll.

The other two stones she put with the cedar bundle. Red jasper, used for protection against spirits and astral attacks, she put in the sand next to the red candle. Yellow jasper, used to protect and strengthen the mind and ward against charms, was placed next to the candle at the east. The extra jasper stones were added to the extra unakite. The large Petoskey stone provided by the owl was placed in the west next to the blue candle because it represented water, emotions, help from the Ancestors, and strength. She placed a small twig of cedar next to the candle that sat in the north to represent the stability and longevity of earth.

The lake water was last. Ashlynne uncorked the bottle and, pouring a small amount into her hand, she walked clockwise around her suite, sprinkling the water to connect each candle to the next. As she walked, she could see a frothy dark blue line shimmer and dance along the hardwood floor between each compass point.

Ashlynne concentrated on the energy and power of the lake and sent the energy into the circle she was creating around the perimeter of her rooms. When she felt its power settle, she lit the end of the dried cedar and blew on it to release the fragrant smoke. Again, moving clockwise, she wafted the smoke from the smudge stick around the circle, sealing the protective barrier. When she felt confident that she had created a secure space, she opened the closet door and blew the smoke into the crowded space for good measure—and sent a silent thank you to Michele for helping her learn the basics of this skill. The extra stones she sat on her dresser, and she reminded herself to find a small bag for them.

She would need all the help she could get.

Her last task before attending her duties as the House Manager was to light the candles and activate her circle of protection.

Moving clockwise—Michele had told her once to always move clockwise to create something and counterclockwise to undo it— she began with the candle to the east. Reading from her notes, she moved from candle-to-candle whispering, "Creature of Fire, work your will at my desire. Fire jump and fire flame and fire do as I proclaim: Protect this space and all within—Murphy, Meredith, and Ashlynne are three—as I say, so mote it be."

By the time Ashlynne reached the candle in the west, she could feel for the first time the energy within the doll stir. By the time she completed her chanting at the northern candle, she had a clear vision of Meredith and could feel the powerhouse that was her spirit.

"Wow! I wonder if Dark Grove has any idea of what it's getting into!" said Ashlynne to her dog as the strength of Meredith's energy rippled out from the closet only to bounce back into the suite of rooms as it hit the barrier of the magical circle Ashlynne had so carefully set.

Ashlynne could see Meredith's energy as ropes of dark green with gold coiling shot out from the closet like whips, strong and incessant. She was confused when the emotion coming from the display of energy was one of approval rather than anger. When the green whips hit the circle's edges and could go no further, she thought it was more likely that Meredith would be irate to find herself both imprisoned within the doll and now captured within a magical circle. It took a minute or two of Ashlynne stilling herself enough to reach out and attempt to communicate to realize that Meredith had tested and approved of the circle's construction.

"You're welcome," Ashlynne whispered as

she saw the pine-colored energy move back into the closet where Meredith was hidden.

The antique Tiffany grandfather clock in the main foyer boomed, signaling the noon hour and making Ashlynne jump.

"Just four more hours until they're here, Murphy! It's time to prep the rest of the house."

Ashlynne snuffed out the lit candles and, reading the instructions provided by Mimi, carefully cut a door within her magical circle that allowed her and the dog passage without breaking the spell. Once Murphy was out, she sealed the magical barrier and closed the physical door to her suite.

The rest of the afternoon was spent straightening the beds and laying out fresh towels. There was no need to make the beds fully; the housekeepers had visited during the last few days, readying the rooms for the guests. Ashlynne and Murphy added small welcoming touches—towels folded and arranged with small artisan soaps placed onto each bed, vases of fresh flowers on each dresser, and fancy bottled water with cut crystal glasses provided at each bedside. One or two small chocolates from Kilwin's, an amazing candy shop located downtown, were added to the bedsides, and completed the cozy and welcoming tableau in each room.

"I would love to arrive to something so pretty!" Ashlynne remarked to Murphy as they finished the last of the bedrooms.

"Let's finish the kitchen and then I can shower and get ready for whatever is headed our way," she said to the small terrier at her heels.

The kitchen was wiped down and swept, and her personal groceries were relocated to the lower-level catering kitchen so the delivery of the guests' food could be placed within the main refrigerator and cabinets.

Upon arranging her food in the smaller kitchen, Ashlynne was delighted to see that a plain old drip coffee maker sat on a counter—with a timer!

"Yay!" she smiled at Murphy who wagged his tail at his human's obvious delight.

From that point on, the young woman and her dog moved from the lowest level and up through the public rooms on the main floor and through the next two floors, switching on sconces, porch lights, and bedside lamps as they went.

"Where's Eliza?" mused Ashlynne as she clicked on the lamp next to the bed in the final guest bedroom.

She and Murphy made it to the third floor, and the proximity to the roof meant the rain and wind were deafening.

"Usually, the lights and lamps are her thing."

Murphy tilted his head, but Ashlynne was already moving down the stairs that led to the second floor and their rooms.

Standing still and gathering her strength,

Ashlynne whispered the incantation that allowed her passage into her rooms without breaking the protective circle she had so carefully constructed.

"Time to get cleaned up, Murphy. The Witches are coming."

Chapter 16

Stella sat staring blankly out the window of the backseat of the car as it traveled from the nondescript house on a nondescript bay along the back roads of Northern Michigan. The highway ran through the rural countryside of open farmland and dense pine forests. Enormous homes set back within the trees awaited the last of the extended family members that would arrive to fill the many rooms. Cousins and grandparents, sisters and brothers, family dogs, and the occasional goldfish in a bowl would all settle in for the annual communal gathering of far-flung family, home to roost and celebrate its rarefied and privileged lifestyle.

The sour taste of jealousy flooded her mouth, and Stella swallowed reflexively. That lifestyle should have been hers, and the pain and anger at having her birthright ripped from her felt as sharp now as they had a decade ago when her family stood against her, effectively removing her from its ranks.

As the car hummed along the pavement and one field of greenery flowed into the next, Stella settled into the drive and allowed her mind to wander. The scenery outside blurred and grew indistinct, and she gathered glimpses of the approaching destination: a mansion of gleaming white with pillars and balconies galore, decadent gardens, and sumptuous rooms within. She concentrated on the interior and mentally wandered through room after room, searching for the doll that would provide her with enormous power and the type of house and lifestyle that had always rightly been her own.

The going was not easy, and Stella felt the

first stirrings of concern. There were spaces that she simply could not see through. She knew there were rooms beyond the doors that were visible in her mind's eye. Try as she might to enter them, time and again she was blocked by a wall of energy so dense that she wondered if her visions were false. Added to the images was the very active spirit of a woman who wandered the floors continuously picking up this and that, watering plants, switching lamps off and on—always walking-walking-walking. Stella was sure she had not encountered such a peculiar home in all her life. She was glad to have the whole group with her for this chore. The energy within Rosehaven was chaotic and would take some time, once she arrived, to understand who was who and what was what.

As Stella continued her mental tour of Rosehaven, her consciousness flowed into a large kitchen, and she was slammed with the brightest light she had ever encountered. Pulling back to gather herself, she carefully moved forward again, blocking out as much of the light as possible.

She was able to make out the source of the light: a young woman, a few years her junior with copper-colored hair braided over one shoulder, who was talking to a small dog as she set pastries and fresh fruit into large baskets lined up along the center of an enormous butcher block farmhouse style table. The young woman shone like a halogen lamp and adding to her light were the sparks emanating from the key-shaped scar on her dog's forehead.

"Well, doesn't this just get more and more interesting?" Stella whispered as she came back to herself and the car that moved steadily into the maelstrom that was Rosehaven.

Ashlynne filled the last of the baskets set out along the length of the kitchen table that would welcome Dark Grove to Rosehaven. As she set the last piece of fruit into the final basket, the hairs on the back of her neck and along her arms prickled painfully as she became aware of something or someone peeking around the door jamb from the butler's pantry behind her. Slowly, she turned to look at Murphy so she could get a stealthy glance at the doorway.

From the corner of her eye, she could see the watery image of a woman who looked to be a few years older than her. While petite, the woman was still a good six inches taller than Ashlynne, and her mahogany curls were midnight dark compared to Ash's copper-penny waves. Once again, the image flickered in and out of view like a picture from an old tube television, zigging and zagging out of focus the longer Ashlynne looked at it.

The woman with dark ringlets was peering

around the door frame into the kitchen, but every few seconds another image superimposed itself over her. Gone was the petite dark-haired woman, replaced by a wraith with sickly gray skin, obscenely red lips, and talon-like fingernails to match. Its eyes were slits that gleamed with both interest and amusement, and its hair appeared as dry as corn husks but black as pitch. When the specter realized that Ashlynne had noticed its presence, its red-lipped mouth split in a monstrous grin showcasing amazingly white teeth and a set of upper canines that appeared to have been filed into deadly points.

Just as Ashlynne was beginning to break and run for the backyard, rain and thunder be damned, the grotesque creature winked out of view, leaving the human woman who had stepped back from the doorway and had her arm up to shield her eyes. Unsure as to who this was or what she was shielding herself from, Ashlynne turned around to face her fully—only to find that she was gone.

"What the hell was that?" gasped Ashlynne as her legs gave out, and she sat down in a heap on the hardwood floor of the kitchen.

"Did you see them, Murphy?" she asked her dog who had come to sit on her lap.

He had also seen the visitors, and more to the point, he recognized the scent of the red-lipped monster. While it traveled far and wide in this world, it held the scent of the Fae—a realm that Murphy would never forget. He buried his head under Ashlynne's arm, comforting both himself and his mistress. He understood that something from that place had found them again, and it scared him a great deal.

Ashlynne lost track of how long she and Murphy sat, lost in thought, on the kitchen floor when the chiming of the Tiffany clock announced that it was four o'clock. Picking herself up and brushing dust from her pants, she heard the slam of a car door just as the lights throughout Rosehaven began turning off and on erratically.

"Is Eliza welcoming the guests or warning us of their arrival?" wondered Ashlynne in a near whisper as Murphy whined and moved closer to her legs.

"I'm guessing it's a warning to be on the safe side, given what we already know about these people from Mimi," she whispered to the terrified dog at her feet.

"We're stronger and we have the upper hand, Murphy. They don't know that we know why they're here. We can do this; I know we can."

But Murphy wasn't so sure. Most of what his human said was true, but he didn't think she realized or understood where the thing with the long fingernails had come from. And while he did know, he didn't yet have an understanding as to why it was here and what it wanted. That would come, though, and was what scared him the most.

Chapter 17

Ashlynne measured ground coffee into the filter-lined basket and set the pot to brew as she yawned loudly. The sun hadn't risen yet, but her mornings began early so she could attend her duties as House Manager and still avoid the members of Dark Grove as much as possible. As the smell of the dark roast coffee filled the large kitchen, she removed the plastic that covered the scones and bagels that she had purchased the day before from the small bakery on Antrim Street downtown.

Arranging the delicate baked goods onto a large platter, she added it to the other items spread down the center of the kitchen table;

fresh fruit, small containers of yogurt, and bowls of granola and jam completed the array of offerings for the guests' continental breakfast. Finally, she put mugs, spoons, cream, and sugar alongside the coffee maker and a chilled pitcher of orange juice next to that, and she was finished for the time being.

Trudging down the stairs to the smaller catering kitchen where her personal items were now stored, Ashlynne poured her coffee and prepared Murphy's kibble and pumpkin. As the tiny terrier ate, she nibbled on a raspberry and lime scone and pondered the last week.

Dark Grove arrived during the worst early-summer storm in the town's memory, an event that Ashlynne didn't think was a coincidence. Their entry literally blew the heavy front door in, bringing with them sheets of driving rain, fern fronds that had been ripped from their base by the high winds, and spinning whirlwinds of maple and oak leaves. The group hadn't seemed to notice or care and took their time wheeling their luggage into the foyer and closing the door against the fury of the elements. The guest named Stella seemed to welcome the storm, a fact that later Ashlynne would realize was part and parcel of the woman's energy, making her both strong and chaotic—a storm in and of herself.

Ashlynne greeted the group that day with her best waitress voice and smile, all the while cringing inside with the knowledge of who they really were and why they were at Rosehaven. A moment of panic almost caused her to completely break down when, as she was escorting the group up the main staircase to their rooms on the second and third floors, she saw that while she had removed the doll from its pedestal in the music room, she had left the space empty. To her, the unadorned table screamed that something was terribly wrong, though the members of the group hadn't seemed to notice the empty space at all. In truth, Rosehaven was so luxuriously decorated that, at one's first visit, the house's effect could be a bit overwhelming. That seemed to be the case with Dark Grove based on the whispered oohs and ahhs as they climbed the stairs and were shown to their rooms.

Ashlynne had chosen to lead the group to the third floor first, depositing the only couple in one of the adjoining rooms with their suitemate being a solitary man. Another single man was let into his suite at the end of the hall before leading the remaining three individuals to the second floor.

"This room should be perfect for you," smiled Ashlynne as she led Stella to the room furthest from her own, an overly feminine room dripping with cream-colored lace and mink stoles draped over the back of a damask-covered slipper chair. Two twin beds piled with more damask and heavy cream-colored velvet coverings occupied the center of the room and tucked under the eaves was a small private bathroom.

"I think I'd rather have that one," suggested Stella, pointing to the room across the hall and directly beside Ashlynne's suite. It shared a bathroom with the room next to it, but more importantly, the rooms on that side of the house shared balconies. The room that Stella chose had direct access to Ashlynne's.

Trying to keep her smile in place and not visibly balk, Ashlynne nodded and led the woman across the hall to her desired room.

Before entering, Stella stopped and turned to look at Ashlynne's door, "Oh, look! We'll be neighbors!"

Confident that she had not told anyone in the group which suite belonged to her, Ashlynne smiled blandly and showed Stella into the bedroom that she would occupy for most of the summer.

"Let the games begin," she muttered

ruefully as she escorted the other guests to the remaining bedrooms and returned downstairs to set out the wine and cheese for the evening.

After arranging the cheese, crackers, fruit, and a selection of wines, Ashlynne hurried into the music room and plopped a large fern—rescued from the garden where it had landed after being blown off the porch in the storm—onto the decorative table that once held the doll that now resided in her closet.

The footsteps above her head brought her back to the present, and Ashlynne listened closely to the guests who had come down for coffee and pastries. From the sound of it, the entire group was present. Very quietly, she picked up her dog, walked softly through the catering kitchen, and turned to go up the back stairwell. Slipping quickly out the service door, she led Murphy down the sidewalk to the public beach access next to Rosehaven, so he could go to the bathroom away from the group that now held sway in their usual morning location.

Even after a week of their company, Ashlynne couldn't get over the feeling that the paying guests were, in fact, intruders and interlopers, and it made it difficult to maintain her happy, House Manager face.

Lake Michigan rolled into the shore, serene in its majesty. Its deep blues and vibrant greens rivaled any Caribbean beach, save for its temperature. While June was proving to be pleasantly warm, the waters of the immense lake remained at a chilly 50-some degrees at the shore, if not downright frigid further out, and acted as a natural air conditioner for the areas closest to the shore.

Ashlynne watched as small family groups and solitary retirees wandered the early-morning beach, toes digging into the wet sand. Every few yards, someone stopped to pick up a stone or examine a feather, and it did Ashlynne's heart good to know that other people were arriving in the small town, and more every day. Though it could realistically house double the number of people that were currently in residence, Ashlynne felt both terribly alone and crowded out of the space at Rosehaven. It was a strange feeling to be both responsible for, and at the same time, removed from the place. Observing the arrival of more and more summer visitors helped her to feel less alone.

When he had finished his business and had some time to enjoy the summer sunshine, Ashlynne led Murphy back to Rosehaven. By now it was time to straighten the bedrooms, clean up the kitchen, and start the laundry. Once the housekeepers arrived, she could check and, if need be, reinforce the wards that kept her suite and its occupants safe.

Chapter 18

Ashlynne sat cross-legged in front of the mirror, gaping wide-eyed at Mimi, and scrambling to take notes to remember the latest batch of information that the spirit was imparting. She would absolutely need to remember this. Everything.

"So, why am I just hearing about this now? Why didn't you tell me about the stone when you first told me about the doll?" Ashlynne asked.

"It's a lot of information to take in and process, Dear. I thought it best to give you what you needed step by step," replied Mimi who was pacing back and forth from one side of the mirror to the other and smoking like a chimney.

"You're scared, aren't you?" asked Ashlynne as she watched the normally implacable woman move back and forth repeatedly; smoking, talking, smoking, walking.

"Nonsense, Ashlynne. I just want to make sure that you know and understand all that needs to be done and in the precise order; there will not be a second chance to get this right," Mimi warned.

"You're scared," Ashlynne repeated, now frightened as well.

"Alright, I'm a little concerned, but not scared. Feeling scared is a luxury that we aren't allowed," Mimi answered.

Ashlynne looked down and consulted her written notes to hide her face, sure that her expression of fear would not be appreciated by Mimi who had taken on the tone of a military sergeant sending rookie troops into battle. All in all, it was not a comforting display.

"So, now that I've hidden and protected the doll to keep the members of Dark Grove from reaching it, I need to find a stone that Stella has, and this stone will set Meredith free from the doll? What is it with all these stones, anyway?" muttered Ashlynne into her notebook.

"Stones have a magic all their own, Dear. And they're practical; they can hide in plain sight like on a beach, by the side of a road, or on a guest's dresser. Despite being nondescript, they hold the magic and energy of all the elements—earth, fire, water, air— because it takes all those forces to craft, shape, form, and smooth the rocks and stones that we gather. People like you and the members of Dark Grove know how to pull the elemental energy necessary from each to perform your needed tasks."

"I am nothing like the people in Dark Grove!" Ashlynne cried, defensively.

"Oh, but you are. You can see, feel, manipulate, and direct energy just like they can."

"But they've done terrible things!"

"They've done things in pursuit of power and control rather than working in harmony with energy," Mimi added.

"How can someone manipulate energy and, at the same time, work in harmony with it?" Ashlynne asked the pacing spirit.

"Energy follows the path of least resistance, Dear. Knowing how energy normally moves allows for a harmonic relationship with it. Manhandling natural forces and smashing them into a box that has been artificially crafted for one's one purposes is not harmony," Mimi explained.

"Like trapping someone inside a doll?"

"Yes, like trapping someone inside a doll. Are you beginning to understand now, Ashlynne?"

"A little. Mimi?"

"Yes, Dear?"

"Am I a Witch?"

The spirit paused, "Such a charged word, Witch. I suppose to some you might be. And to others, you would be a psychic, a seer, a mystic, or a mage. Labels can be a blessing or a bane, Ashlynne; choose yours wisely."

Mimi dragged her favorite wooden chair into view from the edge of the mirror's frame. Ashlynne had learned that it was Mimi's let's get down to business chair and straightened up herself, ready for more lessons and instructions. As much as she hated to admit it, she was glad that Mimi had parceled out the information; to be hit with all of this at the beginning would have been too much.

"OK," declared Ashlynne, consulting her notes. "I need to continue to protect my suite, and I need to find the stone that Stella has so I can release Meredith from the doll."

"The Journey Stone, Ashlynne. It's called a Journey Stone," Mimi corrected.

"Yes, OK—the Journey Stone," Ashlynne repeated as she made note of the correct name in her notebook.

"And this stone, the Journey Stone, is a brown-green colored rock with a band of quartz going around its whole shape with no breaks, right?"

Mimi exhaled three perfectly shaped smoke rings and replied, "Yes. It's important that the band of quartz does not have any breaks, if it does, then it is not a Journey Stone."

"Wait, are there more than one of these?" Ashlynne asked.

"Oh, yes, Dear. Just like there are more than the unakite you collected. But you will need the specific Journey Stone that Stella used."

Ashlynne stared at her friend, eyes wide and mouth open, "Mimi?"

"Yes, Dear?"

"What if Stella or the other members of the

coven have more than one of these stones? How will I know which one is the correct one?"

"Oh, I have no doubt that you'll figure that out, Dear," encouraged Mimi.

And with her final encouraging words, Mimi stubbed out her cigarette and walked out of view.

Ashlynne fell back against the pillows scattered on the floor with a loud grumble and stared at the ceiling that soared fourteen feet overhead.

"That woman is insufferable! How in the world am I supposed to figure out which is the right stone if there are multiples?"

Murphy, hidden in a nest of blankets, poked his head out and whined at Ashlynne, the tone of her voice alerting him to trouble.

"I guess we'll just have to hope that there isn't more than one Journey Stone, huh, Murph?" she asked the nestled dog.

Murphy extricated himself from his pile of

blankets and sat beside Ashlynne who was reading the rest of her notes.

"I guess the first thing is to find out where Stella has hidden the stone we need. And for that, we might need yet another stone—imagine that!"

Her laughter held a sharp edge of sarcasm laced with fear, but Murphy had trotted out into the hall and into the bedroom, and Mimi was no longer in the mirror, so no one was around to hear it or care.

Ashlynne stood up, gathered her notes, and joined Murphy in the bedroom. The mid-June sunshine filtered through the lace curtains at the French doors, and Ashlynne resented how having Stella next door inhibited her ability to freely open the doors to the lake or to use her side of the balcony without worry. Despite her concerns, she desperately wanted to stand on the balcony to breathe in the fresh air and think.

Sighing heavily, she stashed her notes

under the t-shirts in the dresser and stood in front of the French doors. Closing her eyes, she breathed in deeply and exhaled the fear and anxiety that pooled in her chest. Feeling a new sense of calm, she felt outward, trying to catch a glimpse of anyone who might be on the balcony. Images bloomed in her mind: empty settees and lounge chairs, large pots filled with geraniums and ivy, the neighboring French doors closed, and curtains pulled shut.

She smiled and opened her eyes.

"It's safe, Murphy. No one else is out there or even in their rooms."

Ashlynne and Murphy spent a lazy afternoon on the balcony lounging in the sun and enjoying the lake breezes. While Murphy had no problem falling fast asleep in the mild June air, Ashlynne could feel disapproval coming in waves from the full-length mirror in her sitting room. Apparently, Mimi did not think a break in the sun was an acceptable way to end their conversation. Taking a sip from her water bottle, Ashlynne sent a smile back to the disapproving spirit.

"Don't worry, Mimi," she said, certain her friend could hear, "We'll get to work in just a little bit. I seriously need this sunshine, though."

As Ashlynne closed her eyes and floated away into the sounds of the lake, the breeze, and the occasional rumble of a car passing the house, she heard Mimi say,

"Alright, Dear. But don't be too long. There's a lot to do and not a lot of time to do it."

Ashlynne did her best thinking while floating between sleep and wakefulness, and today was no exception. As the lake and the wind provided a comforting backdrop of white noise, Ashlynne's brain was busy rifling through the images, instructions, and impressions from her most recent conversation with Mimi. By the time she roused herself, she had decided on the best way to try to locate the Journey Stone that Stella had used to trap Meredith in the doll.

"Murphy! C'mon! Let's go," she said to the still-sleeping dog as she nudged him awake.

"We've got things we need to do for Rosehaven before we can try to find Stella's Journey Stone."

Ashlynne walked back inside with Murphy trailing unenthusiastically behind her. As she closed the door to the balcony, she silently congratulated herself for extending her magic circle out to her section of the balcony. Using the incantation to open and close the circle each time they entered and exited had become tedious.

The sun was moving toward the horizon as Ashlynne slipped silently down the service stairs to ready the evening wine and cheese selection for Dark Grove. She had left Murphy in the bedroom, much to his annoyance, because she wanted to complete this chore as quickly as possible.

Gathering the wedges and wheels of cheeses from the refrigerator, along with a bunch of purple grapes and some strawberries, Ashlynne hastily arranged everything on a platter and set it in the butler's pantry next to the wine cooler and bar. She fanned out cocktail napkins, added crackers to a cut glass bowl, and made sure that the ice maker had a full bin of cubes. After dumping mixed nuts into a cloth-lined basket and moving a small vase of fresh flowers closer to the arrangement, she finished her task.

The voices of the coven members could be heard chattering away as they descended the grand staircase just as Ashlynne was running up the service stairs on the other side of the wall.

Quickly muttering the incantation that allowed her into her suite without breaking the protective magic, she closed the door, repeated the verse again to close the circle, and sat down on her bed to catch her breath.

"OK, Murph—I'm done. Let's go see what the town looks like in the summer. This seems like a good evening to go find a burger and fries. What do you think?" she asked.

The small terrier danced and twirled on his back legs as she slipped his harness over his head and clipped the leash into place. Grabbing her wallet and her phone, Ashlynne repeated the protective ritual and carried Murphy quietly down the stairs and out the side door.

As she turned right and walked toward downtown Charlevoix, Ashlynne turned to look back at Rosehaven; the Dark Grove Coven was gathered in the kitchen, and she could see and hear them from the large windows that were cranked open to allow the evening breezes in. Their voices floated out to the sidewalk, sounding strangely normal given the purpose of their visit. Just as she started to turn away, another figure stepped up to the window. Ashlynne stopped dead in her tracks.

Standing directly at the window, the figure had her hands and one cheek pressed flat against the screens with her face turned so that her left eye was peering directly at Ashlynne. The nails on the figure's splayed fingers were long and razor-sharp. As Ashlynne watched, the specter drew her fingers into claws, causing the screens to split where its nails dragged against them. Its smile widened and pointed teeth could be seen glinting in the streetlights that blinked up and down Michigan Avenue. The coven chatted on, oblivious to the creature that was standing right in their midst.

"Oh, Murphy! How could they not know? How could they not see it?" whispered Ashlynne as she and the dog hurried down the darkening street toward the safety of the brightly lit stores and restaurants just a few blocks away.

"I don't know about you, but I am in no hurry at all to go back into the house. Why hasn't Mimi said anything about this thing? And come to think of it, why haven't I thought to ask her? I've already seen it once; it was watching us just before the coven arrived. How could I have forgotten that?" she wondered.

Crossing the bridge and entering the shopping district, Ashlynne slowed her pace and her breath. While she no longer felt hungry, running pell-mell through the small town didn't seem like a good idea—best to blend in a little. Walking calmly would help them fit in and might slow her heart that was threatening to break free from her chest. Truth be told, the specter with its pointed teeth and long fingernails frightened her a great deal.

As Ashlynne and Murphy caught their breath and walked slowly down Bridge

Street, the small town's summer vibe felt infectious. Ashlynne smiled with delight and amazement at the difference between the deserted streets and shops she saw a few weeks ago and the hustle and bustle of the town now. People walked shoulder to shoulder along the narrow sidewalks, and cars idled bumper to bumper on the street as the influx of visitors tested the small town's roadways and lack of stoplights.

She looked at the large crowds crammed into the restaurants and felt positive that none would allow her dog inside. She backtracked to the bridge and took the stairs down to the promenade that ran along the Pine River Channel. She had discovered this lovely path a few days ago and was told there was a small cafe at the end of it—tonight was the perfect time to check it out.

The channel's waters shone darkly below the painted guard rails, and the reflections of the condominiums' lights acted as star-like counterpoints to the inky ribbons of water flowing under the bridge. Compared to the crowds and traffic on Bridge Street, it was quiet and serene along the water. A little further on, with the lighthouse growing larger and larger as she approached, Ashlynne turned left off the cement walkway, forcibly dragging Murphy away from a small container of worms left from someone's afternoon of fishing.

Lake Michigan was kicking up evening waves to their right as they wandered past an ancient playground half-buried in the sand and to their left a massive stone edifice with a sign declaring it a DNR Fishery Station. Ashlynne stared in surprise as she rounded a gentle curve in the sidewalk to see crowds and crowds of people, even more than were on Bridge Street. Every inch of the beach wall was taken up with couples and groups sat facing the water and the setting sun. A man on stilts teetered by causing Murphy to tilt his head quizzically. Gaggles of teenage girls in matching sweatshirts with CHARLEVOIX emblazoned across their shoulder blades sauntered past, content knowing that they were being watched by every teenage boy perched on the beach wall.

Vintage muscle cars cruised by slowly, looping up and around the circular drive that encompassed the park sitting just off the beach.

"Wow, Murph! Who would've thought that all these people were down here? Especially since so many are still downtown! I had no idea that this town got so busy!" she exclaimed.

Murphy, however, was more interested in dinner than cars and people. He tilted his head back, nose in the air, and gathered in the smells of burgers, fries, and ice cream that wafted from the small building sitting in the center of the park. Constructed of the same stone as the Fishery Building and adorned with flower-filled planters and hand-lettered menus, the small cafe looked cheery and welcoming. Surprised to see that the only occupant of the patio was a lone person strumming a guitar, Ashlynne and Murphy approached the window and placed their order. Or—rather—Ashlynne placed their order, though Murphy knew one of the burgers was absolutely for him.

They took a seat on the cobblestone patio and watched the circus of people and cars a few yards in front of them. As the sun moved closer and closer to the horizon and seagulls laughed and wheeled above them, Ashlynne thought that she had never seen such a beautiful place in her life.

Chapter 19

Stella sat on the back porch sipping a cup of coffee and watching the gardener finish weeding the individual beds that the network of boxwood hedges created within the knot-work design. The lake breezes blew through the pine trees that lined the back of the garden, the demarcation line that signified the beginning of the steep cliff that led down to the beach below.

Her mind wandered as she mulled over the prospects of finding the doll that imprisoned Meredith. Meredith, who had caused all this trouble with her insistence on balance and honor. Both ideologies were all well and good, but what value did either have without power? The difference in ideologies instigated many arguments and debates that went round and round with no resolution—Meredith insisting that balance and honor would bestow power and Stella insisting that power came from strength, not some fluffy-bunny, witchy version of chivalry.

And while the two women fought and argued their own points of view, both formidable in their own right, the rest of the coven had watched and eventually took sides.

Stella watched as a crow flew overhead, remembering the months of tense interactions within a group that used to act as one. The magic of the group mind had turned toxic, and Stella blamed Meredith for refusing to take the reins and lead.

"No power, no strength, no will," she muttered into her coffee mug.

So, Stella took control. The seven members that stood with her had helped her cleanse the remaining members from the group. Some left willingly, fed up with and afraid of what had been wrought with the fight for leadership. Others seemed determined to stay and continue to support Meredith.

She smiled as she recalled the powerful magic that was used to expunge the disloyal—ritual blades flashing in the firelight as the energy used to cut and sever alliances was sent out, her wolf that hunted and haunted the dreams of those who dared to stand against her, and the simple and extremely effective use of shunning those who tried to remain friends but who's hearts remained with Meredith.

As far as Stella was concerned, you were either one hundred percent with her or you were an enemy; there was no middle ground. Power and strength sit at the extremes, and those who sat in the middle, attempting to play at balance, were weak. She had no use for them. In the end, it left only Meredith against the Dark Grove Coven, and she became its enemy. After naming an enemy, the new group mind grew strong and powerful, though no less toxic. The Witches that now swam within its consciousness knew nothing else and therefore did not recognize the poison that they themselves had brewed.

"What are you thinking about?" asked a voice, interrupting Stella's daydreaming.

Stella was jolted from her thoughts as Camryn sat down on the settee to her right. Though there was room on the one that Stella occupied, Camryn was careful to give the woman her space. Camryn's deference appealed to Stella and allowed the younger woman to rise within the ranks of the group to become the leader's confidant and, at times, spy.

"Good morning," nodded Stella.

She was careful to walk a fine line between approachable yet powerful and distant. She had perfected it and used it now almost without thought.

Stella answered, "I'm thinking of the best way to locate the doll. Our scrying and my wolf told us that, without a doubt, it had been brought here, but the woman acting as the House Manager seems to have been able to hide it—both physically and magically. I have no idea how this has happened, but we're now several weeks into our stay and we're running out of time to find it."

"Are you concerned that Meredith will get away?" Camryn asked.

"Well, she can't get too far away unless she learns how to make the doll walk!" laughed Stella.

Camryn tried to hide her flinch from the brittle anger that the laugh held.

"Yes, I know but—"

"NO," Stella interrupted, "Meredith will not get away. She is here somewhere, and she is still trapped inside the doll. I need to find the doll and destroy it so that she can't cause any more trouble for us."

Privately, Camryn thought it was unlikely that Meredith, while imprisoned within a doll, could cause trouble for anyone. However, she had noticed how the rest of the group had rallied to the call of an enemy. It was an effective technique that not only doubled down the group's devotion to its leader but infused the group mind with excitement and purpose. Camryn had no thoughts one way or the other about whether this was the right or wrong way to lead the coven; she was more interested in maintaining her position of favor so she would never be on the receiving end of the magic they had worked against her former friends. Camryn's goal was simple — survival.

"So, what do you propose?" Camryn asked.

Stella smiled. It was devoid of warmth but full of determination.

"I think it's time we put the screws to Miss Ashlynne. I'm done buying her innocent

House Manager persona. She has somehow managed to hide a doll that we, ourselves, have enchanted. That is just unacceptable. I don't know how she got here and who trained her, but we are stronger than one little redhead, that's for damn sure."

"Oh! I agree completely! We—you—are so much more pow—"

"Oh, for god's sake, stop. I am not interested in validating you, so stop groveling. We have work to do. Get the others, we need to get this settled," Stella demanded and dumped her cold coffee into the fern next to her and left Camryn, her face flushed with embarrassment and shame, to gather the others.

"Meet me in the living room in an hour!" Stella called back over her shoulder as the screen door to the sunroom slammed shut behind her.

Camryn climbed the stairs to the second floor then the third where she knocked on the door where Rose and Nathan slept. Rose and Nathan were the only traditionally married couple in the group, something that they held over the others—in the false belief that the others cared. They did not.

"Hey, you two! Stella wants us in the living room in one hour—robes and cords! If you need coffee or food ahead of time, you'd better hurry!" Camryn called to the door.

Moving on to the next door without waiting for an answer from either of the two occupants, she repeated her announcement. This room had been assigned to Michael, and knowing him, there was no telling if he was alone or if another person, or two, were in the room as well. Making her announcement again, Camryn moved on. She honestly didn't care if anyone heard her; it was more advantageous for her if the others didn't show. If she attended the meeting alone, it would make her presence all the more noticeable to Stella.

The last door on the third floor had been assigned to Benette. The room was described as 'the Girls' Dorm' in their rental agreement and was decorated in pinks, greens, and creams—a little girl's frilly daydream of gingham and lace and hand-painted furniture. The Girls' Dorm occupied the entire end of the third floor and, while spacious and somewhat charming, gave Camryn the creeps. She had no idea how Bennette could sleep in there, but somehow it was managed.

"Bennette! Robes and cords in an hour in the living room!" she shouted from the hall.

At that, Camryn moved back down the hallway to the stairs and descended to the second floor. She knocked loudly on the door to the room that Riley was in with its double twin beds and explosion of decadent femininity. It didn't surprise Camryn one bit that her sister had chosen this room; it may as well have been decorated with her in mind.

After repeating her call to arms at Riley's

door, she returned to her own room that shared a bathroom with Stella's to change her clothes and apply her makeup. 'Robes and cords' signified a formal ritual, and it was important to Camryn to look the part.

Once Camryn had made a quick sweep of the house, she gave the nod to Stella. The housekeepers, gardeners, and even the annoying House Manager were all gone, so they could begin their ritual undisturbed.

Michael moved the red velvet ottoman out of the center of the room, and the group gathered in a circle in its place. The assembled group, seven in total, no longer looked like typical Northern Michigan tourists.

Each member wore a cotton robe of plain black cinched closed with braided, silken cords that signified their level of accomplishment and importance within the coven; each cord represented one of the three primary levels or degrees. A third-degree Witch had reached the highest level, theoretically. Some of the members had cords that signified specialties that they excelled at such as astral travel, gemstone magics, or creation of thought-forms. These cords were conferred by Stella alone—unlike the degree cords which were part of a strict tradition that even Stella wouldn't alter to suit her needs.

It was no surprise that Camryn held all three degrees and the most specialty cords. She would have been gobsmacked to know that her coven mates didn't for one second believe that she had earned any of them based on her skills alone.

Stella stepped into the center of the circle as the remaining six members closed it around her. The necessary chants and incantations to prepare the space for the ritual had already been done, and Stella was anxious to begin. There was no way to tell how long they would have Rosehaven to themselves.

Grasping the long sword in her right hand

and raising her left over her head, Stella walked clockwise within the circle passing each member of her group. Her position as the High Priestess was declared not only by her place within the circle but also by the animal hide that she wore over her shoulders like a mantle—all in addition to the full complement of cords available to coven members that swung about her hips. Her dark curls were piled atop her head, and her hazel eyes rimmed in kohl. Striding about the circle and wielding the massive ritual sword produced an intimidating picture, indeed, and created a powerful effect that Stella was very much aware of.

Stella finished her incantations to cast the circle and, having reached her starting point, held the sword aloft in both hands, stomped her foot thrice upon the floor, and announced, "This circle is cast and sealed! BE IT SO!"

"So mote it be!" intoned the six others.

Stella handed the sword to Camryn and

walked to the center of the circle and, feet spread wide, raised her arms over her head.

"Guardians of the North, the South, the East, and the West and all ye in the Realm of Faerie! I call ye forth to bring me your power and attend to me now! BE IT SO!"

"So mote it be!" they repeated.

The air changed as it thickened and grew heavy. Camryn could never come up with an adequate description. It wasn't like the heaviness before a storm; it was like the air mimicked a whirlpool, sucking everything down and into itself. She squeezed the hand of Riley who stood at her left and who then squeezed the hand of Michael to her left, and this continued around the circle—a silent reminder to hold the energy that Stella called in. If they faltered, the ritual would fail and there would be hell to pay.

Stella's head dropped back exposing her long neck, and from behind her stretched a long, thin gray arm. The attached hand was adorned with razor-sharp fingernails. The hand caressed Stella's neck lovingly then scratched the white skin drawn taught from the awkward position.

As the long fingernails drew drops of blood, the Faerie's face appeared. It was oblivious to the six Witches who surrounded it, focused completely on the beads of red that it had drawn from Stella. The Faerie leaned in and lapped the blood from the woman's neck, the sound of its tongue raspy in the silent room. The six robed figures stood perfectly still, desperately trying to hold and contain the maelstrom of energy that had brought in the Faerie.

Once the Faerie had lapped the last of the red beads of blood from its host, it stood up, eyes glinting with amusement at the humans that thought they were containing it. It stepped back behind its host and leaned in. Stella shuddered violently and closed her eyes. Seconds later her eyes opened, no longer hazel, but the slanted eyes of the Faerie they had called into their circle.

Riley took a deep breath; she was up.

"Greetings and salutations. We thank you for attending us," Riley welcomed.

The Faerie eyed Riley with interest. This human held great power within, and it intrigued her a great deal.

"The doll has been hidden from us, and we need your help. We have offered you a gift and would like one in return," Riley continued.

Riley knew this was the most dangerous part of the ritual. The Fae did not play by any rules, and how Stella had come to this agreement was a mystery. There was nothing to stop the being that now inhabited her body from either demanding more than what was agreed upon or killing its host outright. The group was completely at its mercy, and Riley seemed to be the only one who knew.

Maliciously, the Faerie grinned at her. All

resemblance to Stella was now gone, even her skin had turned the sickly gray of curdled milk.

"What is it that you want?" it purred.

"We want to know where the doll is hidden," replied Riley with what she hoped was the appropriate balance of bravado and respect.

"The doll resides within the Rose, hidden well by one who knows. To steal it back and claim your win, the light that shines must be dimmed."

The Faerie recited the information in a cloyingly sing-song voice, an evil child reciting lessons of ill will.

Riley scribbled as fast as she could, careful to write the words exactly as said by the Faerie that was housed within Stella. As she scratched the last word onto the paper, the air pressure broke, and Stella collapsed in a heap. The Faerie was gone.

She set the notebook to the side and

watched the coven's activity following the departure of the entity. Rose and Nathan stepped into the circle to attend to the still comatose Stella while Camryn gathered up the energy that had made the magic circle, sending it back into the ritual sword. Michael handed a glass of water that had been prepared earlier to Rose who held it to Stella's lips. Only Bennette, implacable and inscrutable, stood unmoving. Riley could never get a good read on Bennette, and it made her nervous. In truth, much about the coven made Riley nervous.

Their training and practices were, in the beginning, focused on raising energy and doing magic to honor their Gods and Goddesses. Meredith had trained them all and introduced them to the ways and mechanics of magic and devotion within the circle. Somewhere along the way, Stella had latched onto a single phrase in the complicated circle incantation, "...and all ye in the Realm of Faerie." Things had gone sideways very quickly from that point on.

Stella and Meredith had waged long and heated arguments over the focus and intent of their group; Meredith wanting to maintain the traditional ways of magic and worship with Stella wanting to focus purely on the gathering of energy for personal power through the invocation of the Fae—who's mention under Meredith was merely a formality. Knowingly going against the group's leader, Stella had conjured and called in Fae when Meredith wasn't around. From the beginning, the Fae they now had almost constant contact with answered their call.

Immediately, they had found that, while it would offer its help and power, it required payment. The payment it required was blood. With Meredith at the helm, this scenario would have been unimaginable, but the group working under Stella had moved so far off their original path, small step by small step, that by the time this requirement had become known it seemed to be just another small step to the power they sought. Riley was painfully aware of the baby steps they had all taken, resulting in the madness that now defined their magic. Unsure as to what the others thought and too afraid to go against the group and incur its fury, she remained silent.

Chapter 20

Ashlynne sat drinking her coffee in the small downstairs kitchen while Murphy ate his breakfast. It was still dark outside and darker yet in the lower level of the house where there were no windows. She could hear the pitch of the washing machine change through the dividing wall as it began the spin cycle, moving the load of towels closer to their swap into the dryer and then eventually to be folded and distributed throughout the guests' rooms later in the morning.

She didn't normally sit and wait for the linens to finish, let alone monitor the cycle of the load, but today she had decided to look once again for the Journey Stone. She hadn't forgotten that she needed to find it, but the events in the house had made it either too difficult or dangerous to look on a regular basis. Ashlynne knew that the coven wanted the doll, and the game of cat and mouse they had all played since mid-June had completely exhausted her.

In addition to her unsuccessful search for the Journey the Stone, unrelenting nightmares had made sleep almost impossible. The house had started to react to the energy the Witches had brought as well, and whether it was Eliza, Meredith in the doll, or the house itself meant little to Ashlynne at this point. The non-stop lights flickering on and off, drains and toilets erupting with no reason, and the intruder alarms being set off resulting in the local police department's arrival on the scene had made the normally serene and dignified house a demented circus.

The buzzer sounded and Ashlynne walked around the corner from the kitchen to the laundry room to transfer the load of towels into the dryer and set it to run a full cycle.

Knowing this would give her about an hour, she scooped up Murphy and climbed the back stairs to the sunroom and the French doors leading out to the gardens. Depositing Murphy in the dog run, Ashlynne stood still in the pre-dawn light, breathing in the scents of the beautiful garden—the heavy scent of roses from the bank of rose bushes now in full bloom, the spice of Gerber daisies, the hint of lavender and under it all, the natural note of the house's unique perfume, the scent of the lake both immediately recognizable and yet impossible for her to describe.

Taking one final deep breath, Ashlynne turned and went back inside to set up the daily continental breakfast for the guests. This entire charade had her feeling drained. She watched them like hawks as they watched her in return, to find out if she would lead them to the doll. All the while, she was forced to chat about parks or small towns they should visit, setting up charming wine and cheese boards in the evening and colorful continental breakfasts in the morning. Thank goodness for the housekeepers because Ashlynne didn't think it was possible to keep the charade going on zero sleep and anxiety in overdrive while also straightening up the bedrooms and putting out fresh linens.

Last night, having been jolted out of sleep by a heavy pounding on her door, Ashlynne realized her mistake and how to fix it. She shot a look of both anger and fear at the closed door that was vibrating with each booming knock; anger because she had finally fallen asleep and fear because there was no one physically large enough to create that amount of noise or strike the door with the force necessary to cause it to vibrate like that. Ashlynne was very grateful that her protective circle was holding because whatever was out on the second-floor landing had to be huge.

Murphy snuggled up to her as she sat up in bed, propping the pillows behind her back and switching on the bedside lamp. As her room glowed in a comforting and mellow light, the knockings grew further and further apart until they eventually stopped altogether.

The damage was done, though, and Ashlynne was wide awake. Again. As this had become the norm, she started to prepare. In her sitting room, she had a full stash of snacks, bottles of juice and water, and some fresh fruit.

She no longer liked to leave her suite after dark. While part of her felt guilty leaving the Witches to have free reign of the house that she was supposed to oversee, she reminded herself that she had been brought here under completely false pretenses, and the woman responsible was currently stuck inside a doll that was locked in her closet for its own protection.

At this point, as far as Ashlynne was concerned, all bets were off on job descriptions and duties. It was while choosing between an apple or a cookie that Ashlynne realized her mistake; her job description gave her the excuse to move into and out of all the rooms of the house at will and with no explanation. While the coven members were watching her closely, not one of them would question her entering their rooms to freshen the linens or remake their beds. Especially if the housekeepers weren't around to do it.

Now, Ashlynne recalled her excitement from just a few hours ago after discovering the ridiculously easy solution for searching for the Journey Stone. She shook her head at how obtuse she could be when confronted with both sleep deprivation and fear and vowed to get her head back in the game.

She gathered Murphy from the dog run and carried him upstairs to their suite so she could shower and be dressed before the coven descended to the main kitchen for their breakfast. But first, she needed to send a text to the housekeepers letting them know that they wouldn't be needed for the next couple of days.

As she remade her bed and piled the pillows back in place against the headboard, Ashlynne tried her best to guess how the summer would end. If she couldn't locate the Journey Stone, would she be able to take the doll back to New Orleans with her? Perhaps Michele could figure out how to release Meredith. She knew that she couldn't just leave her there hidden in the closet for who knew how long.

"And then there's the weird creature with the sharp teeth and fingernails. What the hell is that?" she asked Murphy who was watching a spider run for cover under the heavy marble-topped dresser.

"Tonight, without fail, we need to talk to

Mimi about that thing, and we need to come up with a plan B if I can't find the stone."

Murphy, still watching the spider, allowed the very tip of his tail to wag in response because, after all, he was a good boy, and not responding is rude even if he thought his human needed to stop talking and start searching. He had enough of this house, the Witches, and the weird nighttime knockings and banging that kept them both awake.

Ashlynne, seeing that the sun had made its way to the horizon, left her dog staring down at the spider he had found and stepped into the shower. Scrubbing, lathering, and thinking, she went over what she had planned and how she would do it. Sometimes, being a service worker meant that the people you serve don't see you, and sometimes that was a very, very good thing.

Chapter 21

Ashlynne stood in the laundry room in the lower level of Rosehaven folding fluffy white towels and washcloths and piling them into a large wicker basket. From the closet shelves, she grabbed six rolls of toilet tissue, several boxed bars of bath soap, and two cans of disinfectant spray. A large plastic garbage bag was stuffed into the basket next to these items, and she was ready to go.

Hoisting the basket up and resting it on one hip, she smiled to see that Murphy and the two white dogs that stayed on this level were playing chase around the kitchen table. She decided to leave them to it; if he needed her, he knew the layout of the house now and could find her with ease.

Ashlynne heard the coven members in the main kitchen above her and wanted to avoid them at all costs. She walked through the office and up the back service stairs to the third floor. Though she doubted that the Journey Stone was up here, she felt she might as well accomplish actual room service while she was hunting.

Knocking firmly on the door to the Girls' Dorm and announcing loudly, "Housekeeping!" while pushing it open, Ashlynne entered with a brisk, no-nonsense attitude—careful to avoid the attitude of a furtive and scared young woman preparing to burgle the place.

It appeared that Bennette was a neat freak based on the condition of the room; the bed was not only made but made as it should be, the decorative pillows arranged meticulously and the bed skirt pooling precisely at the floor. The wet towels had been placed into the stand-up shower, not tossed onto the wood floors or furniture, and there was no toothpaste in the sink, no water stains on the bathroom vanity, and all personal toiletries were lined up neatly next to the crystal dishes that held swabs and cotton balls.

Ashlynne hung fresh towels and emptied the small trash can before replacing the almost used bar of soap. Seeing nothing else that needed her attention she moved into the bedroom to see if Bennette had any stones lying about.

It very quickly became apparent that Bennette did not leave anything at all 'lying about' and even seemed to have dusted the top of the dresser and nightstand.

"Very odd," muttered Ashlynne as she stood, hands on hips, looking around the space for any personal items that may have been left in clear view. There were none and not ready just yet to begin rifling through the dresser drawers, she switched off the lights and left the strangely immaculate room for the next one down the hall.

By the time Ashlynne had finished with Michael's room and the adjoining rooms that housed Rose and Nathan, she had a much greater appreciation for what the housekeepers achieved daily and sent a promise up to whatever Gods watched over exhausted and unappreciated service workers that she would begin pulling her weight a little more from here on out. The latter two rooms looked more like an extensive struggle had ensued rather than a night spent sleeping.

"Maybe there wasn't much sleeping. I've overheard them all talk about Michael," Ashlynne said to Murphy who had joined her as she was finishing making the beds.

Murphy snuffled in response as he nosed around under the bed, dragging out a stick from the dark depths.

"Give me that, please," said Ashlynne, bending over to retrieve the length of birch from the dog who shot her a wounded look.

"It's not ours and, more importantly, it's not on the list of things we need to find; it stays," she told the terrier firmly, placing the stick on the chaise lounge under the window.

As she straightened up, her eye caught a dark smudge behind the lace curtains. Moving aside the panel, Ashlynne found several stones the size of golf balls on the deep windowsill—each was a different color and made up of a different group of minerals, but every single one of them had a ribbon of quartz running around its circumference in an unbroken band.

"Journey Stones, Murphy!" whispered Ashlynne excitedly as she scooped them up and hid them at the bottom of her laundry basket. She ran into Michael's room and looked behind his curtains—nothing.

Surveying the room, now careful to notice anything hidden in plain sight, she saw that the cabinet that the television sat on had glass-paned doors that closed in small bookshelves. Gently tugging one open and feeling along the sides of the books, lined up like soldiers, her fingers closed around a stone. Pulling it out and holding it up to the window, she saw that this smaller granite piece also had a band of quartz circumventing it.

Ashlynne and Murphy spent a couple more minutes hunting for stones within the two-bedroom suite and its connected bathroom, but they couldn't locate any others. A quick run down the hall and back to Bennette's room also failed to turn up any other stones.

"Well, we have five different Journey Stones now, Murphy. As soon as we check the last of the bedrooms, we'll figure out which one is the one that Stella used to trap Meredith in the doll," Ashlynne decided.

Carrying the basket and supplies down to the second floor, Ashlynne zipped through her room service duties in the uber-feminine twin bedroom—only one bed had been used, and the bathroom wasn't terribly messy. One more Journey Stone was found hidden in a trinket box on the vanity and was stowed at the bottom of the basket with the others.

"That makes six now, Murphy. I have to say, they came prepared to hide the original, didn't they?" remarked Ashlynne to the dog as they walked across the landing and entered the room used by Camryn.

"You have got to be kidding me," Ashlynne moaned as the full disaster of the room became visible.

The bedding sat in a twisted and bunched pile at the bottom of the mattress with the beautiful custom duvet and decorative pillows wadded and piled in a heap in the corner covered in damp towels. Clothing of every type imaginable was scattered and flung over the entire suite and shoes littered the floor. Candy wrappers, empty water bottles, and magazines covered the tops of every dresser and bedside table, and the doors to the balcony were flung wide open, though the window unit air conditioner had been left running at full capacity.

"It's like a twelve-year-old girl has been living here!" said Ashlynne as she surveyed the disastrous scene.

She remembered how the housekeepers were in here, cleaning and tidying every morning, and the thought made the mess even more incredible. She started with the bed, untwisting while pulling the sheets and blankets back up to the headboard and tucking them under the mattress securely. Removing the damp towels from the pile of extremely expensive custom bedding that had been thrown on the floor, she hoisted the heavy duvet back into place and replaced the decorative pillows.

Taking her time now, Ashlynne gathered shoes into matching pairs while looking into corners and under the bedside tables for more

Journey Stones that could be hidden. She shook the wrinkles out of clothes and folded them all neatly, laying them on the bed for Camryn.

"Of course, if the items on the bottom of the piles are a little damp, she'll learn to not throw her wet towels around, huh, Murph?" laughed Ashlynne to the dog who sat watching with barely concealed boredom.

Murphy wanted to go out and explore the beach some more, not play maid to these humans that smelled sharp and brittle, like anger and spite.

Somewhat surprised to not find any stones in Camryn's room, Ashlynne tackled the shared bathroom, putting out the last of the fresh towels, toilet paper, and soap. She added a new can of air freshener since she didn't see one. Next, she entered Stella's room.

While Stella's suite was not the jaw-dropping display of inconsideration that

Camryn's was, it didn't have the neat-as-a-pin order that Bennette's room had. The bed was made hastily, and some clothing was draped somewhat neatly over the small chair that sat in front of an antique writing desk. Makeup and lotions were scattered around the dresser's top, and the lamp had been left on. All in all, it was a completely unremarkable guest's room—except for the huge wicker basket that Stella must have found on the lower level of the house. It could easily hold a bushel of apples considering its massive size, and it was filled to the brim with stones.

"Oh no," moaned Ashlynne, producing a long, drawn-out sound full of crushing exhaustion and overwhelming fear.

Moving closer, she carefully moved the stones at the top of the pile away for a glimpse of the next layer. It seemed that every single stone within the large basket was a Journey Stone. And there had to be hundreds of them piled messily on top of each other.

"Damn it, Murphy. I feel like someone's about to pop out of the closet door and yell checkmate!" She continued with a sigh, "Our job just got a lot more involved."

Ashlynne finished straightening the room, careful to keep her eyes open for any additional stones that Stella may have hidden in this perverse easter egg hunt. She didn't know whether to laugh or cry when she found three more stones, one under a small needlepoint pillow, one behind the lamp on the dresser, and one being used as a doorstop. When she picked up the stone that propped open the heavy wooden door, it immediately swung shut. Surprised that the stone was serving a purpose, Ashlynne found the heavy rubber door wedge and pushed it into place.

"Incredible," grumbled Ashlynne as she added the three stones to the collection in her laundry basket.

The bushel basket of Journey Stones she lugged into her suite felt heavy and awkward as she paused to say the spell that allowed her entry, no longer caring if anyone noticed her search for the stones. After a moment, she left her suite to attend the laundry.

"I feel perfectly foolish, Murphy," she said to her dog as she stuffed damp bath towels into the large washing machine, "They knew all along that I would be looking for the Journey Stone. What an idiot I can be sometimes!"

She dumped the soap and bleach into their labeled reservoirs, punched the buttons to start the correct cycle, and stomped out to the small kitchen. Murphy watched as she bit angrily into a large cookie and thought it was a terrible waste to eat something so wonderful while feeling too angry to enjoy it.

"Alright, Murph—I have had just about enough of this. Tonight, we're going to talk to Mimi about that creepy creature I keep seeing and how Stella and the others knew that I'd search for the Journey Stone."

Stella entered her room and smiled in delight; the basket of stones was gone! She had giggled all week wondering what the housekeepers thought of her placing a bushel basket of beach stones on her bed every morning. She knew it would only be a matter of time before Ashlynne's curiosity would get the better of her and she would service the rooms herself to snoop.

Surprisingly, it was Bennette who had suggested that the redhead knew about the Journey Stone and designed the scavenger hunt. Stella had her doubts but figured that having some fun with Ashlynne couldn't hurt. Regardless, it was highly unlikely that she would find the correct stone.

Stella felt that she was halfway to locating the doll now. Feeling confident that Ashlynne knew about the doll made her search easier. The coven had scoured every inch with the massive Rosehaven and found no hint of the doll. The only place they had not looked was in Ashlynne's suite. She smiled a smile that would have made the blood run cold in several of her coven-mates; she was very much looking forward to searching Ashlynne's suite.

Chapter 22

Ashlynne and Murphy shouldered their way past groups of tourists that wandered idly along Bridge Street, making their way back to Rosehaven. The crowds were thickly populated every day now as people ate, shopped, and lounged in the parks enjoying the idyllic summer afternoons. By this evening, though, it would be much quieter.

Most visitors gathered in several small towns that surrounded Charlevoix to enjoy the Fourth of July fireworks. Charlevoix didn't participate in fireworks on the fourth. Instead, the town saved their fireworks for the annual Venetian Festival, a few weeks out yet.

Locals and second-home residents knew this and would stay in Charlevoix for the evening to enjoy a brief respite from the summer crowds, though some of the larger private homes on the lakes would host fireworks displays for family, and of course, there were the more modest family gatherings with sparklers and cookouts.

As she wandered, she felt as though she walked through a real-life version of a Norman Rockwell painting, complete with red, white, and blue bunting and dogs catching Frisbees. Ashlynne felt both charmed and alone. To know that lurking just below the surface of this picture-perfect facade was a group that would do anything to gather and maintain as much power as possible at any cost made the carefully curated resort town seem suspect. Was it all a cover for a darker interior, or was the dark an anomaly? Ashlynne didn't like feeling this way—suspicious and somewhat bitter—and tried to focus on the happiness playing out along the sidewalks.

"Not everyone can be faking it, can they, Murphy?" she whispered to her dog as they moved through the groups of happily chattering families.

"Maybe it's because, no matter what, I am truly an outsider here. I have no roots, no family, nothing that this town seems to represent. The people here are shiny, and I'm afraid I'm a little too tarnished to fit in on any long-term level," she continued as they stepped onto the sidewalk spanning the drawbridge.

Murphy's ears twitched as he heard crowds of people speaking, but he continued his fast-paced trot stretching the leash to its end. He enjoyed the groups, the smells, and the different voices and wished Ashlynne would walk a little faster.

As they neared the other side of the bridge, officially entering the north side of

Charlevoix, laughter and the tinkle of glasses emanated from the balcony that stretched along the exterior of one of the town's unique stone buildings. The noises grabbed their attention.

The Weathervane Restaurant operated in Charlevoix for almost seventy years, and the building featured whimsical stonework. The gull-wing sweeps of the roof remained a grand testament to the local architect who had designed it.

Many decades in the past, Earl Young had purchased the old grist mill that had ground wheat into flour to be transported throughout the region. The transformation from the mill to a true landmark in the early 1950s was the physical embodiment of a postcard. Signs of the old mill, though, shimmered through the bold stonework here and there like minnows under running water.

Ashlynne could see the rugged, homely building that had provided so much for the early settlers. The images shifted and flickered through to the current time. While it was not nearly the beauty of the creation that currently stood there, the grist mill—with its four stories of boxed symmetry—held its own vintage charm. Ashlynne was sorry that it wasn't visible to everyone.

She stopped just past the bridge and took a picture to send to Andrew and stood watching people lunching and chatting under the umbrellas that shaded each table. The balcony soared over the channel that flowed below, allowing for a bird's-eye view of the pleasure crafts and ferries that floated into and out of Lake Michigan and Round Lake.

As the patrons enjoyed their drinks and specialty entrees, a lone man in a cutaway waistcoat and top hat wandered among the tables, stopping here and there to smile at a pretty young woman or watch a sailboat cruise by below. As Ashlynne watched, he turned suddenly and noticed her watching.

The gentleman, resplendent in his formal attire, smiled broadly and made a sweeping bow, doffing his top hat and setting it back on his head at a jaunty angle meant to impress.

"Isn't he something?" laughed Ashlynne as Murphy tilted his head in response to the man's display.

Images flowed from the spirit to her— rowdy, elegant parties from the late 1800s where men and women, done up in the latest fashions from the east coast, drank champagne and danced on the plain wood-plank floors of a cavernous second-story hall.

"He didn't die at the restaurant, Murphy, but it's the closest place to what he found so enjoyable in his life, so he stays here. The dance hall he showed me is gone, burnt to the ground, but he didn't die in the fire. He died an old man who loved his life so much that he's stayed on this side. He says the staff at the Weathervane know him and don't mind him being there, and that some of them call him Frank, but that isn't his name," she informed Murphy.

As Ashlynne and Murphy watched, the ghost—who was not named Frank—followed a uniformed staff member through the door into the dining room and out of view.

Charmed by the images shown to her of a Charlevoix that used to be, Ashlynne and Murphy continued down the sidewalk and into the now-familiar canopy of trees lining Michigan Avenue. The warmth of the sun was filtered by the maples and oaks and cooled by the breezes off Lake Michigan as they walked the last few blocks to Rosehaven. Ashlynne hoped that the members of Dark Grove were out for the day. She had no more desire to see any of them now than she did earlier in the morning after she found the large basket of Journey Stones. She was angry for feeling foolish earlier.

The driveway was empty without the coven's car, and upon entering the house,

Ashlynne could feel it was empty of living people as well.

"Hello!" whispered Ashlynne into the service entry, and the overhead light flickered briefly in greeting.

She smiled and sent a smile to Eliza then climbed the stairs to her suite. It was time to talk to Mimi and figure out which stone, of the hundreds she had found, was the enchanted Journey Stone needed to free Meredith. She desperately wanted to ask Mimi about the frightening spirit that she had seen hanging around and whether it had anything to do with the Journey Stone, the doll, or the Witch trapped within it.

After whispering the incantation, now done almost completely by rote, Ashlynne opened the doors to her balcony and slipped her tennis shoes off in favor of her flip flops. Murphy scooted under the bed for an afternoon nap while Ashlynne rooted through her stash of snacks and settled on a bag of mini sandwich cookies, a banana, and some water from the bathroom tap. She would make some coffee in a little while but for now, this would do.

"Mimi! We need to talk!" called Ashlynne, her voice slightly muffled around the banana she chewed.

The quiet was so complete that she could hear the neighbors across the street as they gathered for a Fourth of July cookout. She heard good-natured teasing, a dog barking, and the rattle of a grill being wheeled around on the cement from the street below. Still, the mirror remained empty save for the reflection of herself and the sitting room where she currently sat eating her lunch.

"Mimi! C'mon! I don't know how much time I have!" Ashlynne called.

Smoke rings floated from the side of the mirror, bobbing and floating into the center of the glass. Following the smoke was Mimi dragging her chair with a lit cigarette drooping off her bottom lip, uncharacteristic to the spirit's typical appearance.

"Uh, hello?" ventured Ashlynne at the spectacle that her friend presented — Mimi shuffling along, dragging a chair, cigarette dangling like a longshoreman.

Mimi looked exhausted and disheveled, and Ashlynne couldn't begin to imagine what had caused this.

"Hello, Dear," sighed Mimi as she dropped onto the chair.

"What in the world is the matter?" cried Ashlynne, feeling truly alarmed at her friend's appearance and demeanor.

"I'm feeling a little under the weather. That's all,"

"Under the weather? You look a lot worse for the wear than under the weather, Mimi."

"Be that as it may, what can I do for you, Dear?" sighed the spirit.

"Um, well, I found the Journey Stone."

"Well, that's wonderful, Dear. And you

know what to do now, yes?"

"Uh—no, no I don't. See, the problem is that I have found the Journey Stone, but it's hiding somewhere amongst the other one hundred and fifty other Journey Stones that I have also acquired."

"That's just silly, Ashlynne!" snapped Mimi, "Why would you collect so many of them when I told you that all you needed was the one the coven had used to trap Meredith?"

Ashlynne stared gape-mouthed at her friend. She couldn't be serious.

Gesturing widely behind her to the general place where the bushel basket of stones was sitting, she exclaimed, "Mimi! Do you think I would have the time or the inclination to collect a bushel basket of stones, let alone a particular type of stone? No! The answer to that is no. They set me up! They knew that I would be looking for the stone, and they planted about a half dozen decoys. There was

a full damn basket of the cursed things! How
has this happened? How did they know?"

Mimi slumped in her chair, chin resting on
her chest—the picture of exhaustion and
despair.

"They shouldn't have known, Ashlynne.
Please tell me where you found these stones.
Maybe I can solve the mystery if I know how
you came to acquire them."

Ashlynne walked Mimi through that
morning, the supplies she gathered, the state
of the rooms, where she had found the
assorted hidden stones, and then the large
basket full of them that had sat on Stella's
bed.

"Which room required no cleaning?" she
asked once Ashlynne had finished her
account of the morning.

"The first suite I searched. It's called the
Girls' Dorm."

"Yes, but who is staying in that one?"
Mimi pressed.

"Bennette."

"Does this person have another name? Perhaps a first name or a last? Most people do have at least two, Ashlynne."

Narrowing her eyes at the spirit's sarcasm but letting it slide due to the strange state that her friend was in, Ashlynne replied, "I have not heard of another name. Just Bennette. That's all."

"I see," sighed Mimi, lighting another cigarette.

"Well, I don't! What does Bennette have to do with anything, Mimi?"

"Bennette is not a member of the coven. Not really, anyway. Even if he is acting the part right now, it is only an act and makes all this much more dangerous. I'm so sorry I brought you to this house, Ashlynne."

"I don't understand, and you're starting to scare me," whispered Ashlynne.

"Bennette is old, much older than me. If Bennette is here then everything you are doing is known—your awareness of the stone, your abilities and talents, and your friendship with me."

"This sounds bad, Mimi."

"Oh, it's much worse than bad, Dear. If Bennette is here then the Baobhan Sith is here, and that is as bad as it can get, I'm afraid."

"The babo-what?" Ashlynne asked, frightened.

"The Baobhan Sith," the spirit spoke the words slowly, letting the sounds baa'van see resonate with Ashlynne, and continued, "It's a Faerie—of sorts."

Ashlynne, legs crossed in a lotus position, fell backward onto the pillows behind her and groaned.

"You cannot be serious! Another one? Why? How? Didn't Murphy and I just get rid of a Faerie?" she cried.

"You must know that Faerie is a race!" Mimi snapped back, "There are many of them. The traditionally good Faeries, or the

Seelie Court, we don't usually see or interact with because they would prefer we not. They keep to themselves. The traditionally bad Faeries, or the Unseelie Court, are the members of the race that we see more of simply because they want us to. We are playthings to them at best, prey at worst. Of course, none of the Fae are good or evil as humans understand it—some are just worse for us than others."

Ashlynne sat up and took a drink of her water, "So, what is this Baobhan Sith? Why is it with the coven?"

"That is a very good question, and there will be no positive reason for it being here or attached to a group of Witches. The Baobhan Sith is, like I said, part of the Unseelie Court of the Fae. It is one of the only members that drink human blood. If I had to hazard a guess it would be that someone in the coven has compacted with this Faerie. The Witch who established the deal may feel that immense power is bequeathed from their faux alliance, but it is a lie. The Fae do not grant power to humans and if it appears that one has then, rest assured, it will be taken away when the Faerie has had its fill of amusements."

"I've seen a thing lurking around the house, Mimi. It's not a typical ghost found in Rosehaven, and it's really scary. It looks like it could be a pretty woman except for the color of its skin and its horrifying teeth and fingernails. I've seen it twice now," Ashlynne explained.

"So, it is here," sighed Mimi in resignation, "That must be the cause—that's why I am feeling so poorly," she said more to herself than to Ashlynne.

"Why would it make you sick?" asked Ashlynne, afraid to hear the answer.

"Did this lady have sharp teeth like fangs and very long fingernails, Ashlynne?"

"Yes. But why would it—"

"And its feet? Did you see its feet?" asked

Mimi, cutting off Ashlynne's question.

"No, I haven't seen its feet. Mimi, please! Why would this Faerie make you sick?"

"I'll get to that, I promise. But you need to know about this Faerie first. Like I said, it's a blood drinker—"

"Like a vampire?" interrupted Ashlynne.

"Yes and no," continued Mimi, "Yes, it drinks human blood and no, it does not suck blood from its victims as a vampire does."

"Wait, so vampires are real?" interrupted Ashlynne again.

"Do you really have to ask that, Dear? Of course, they are real, but this is not one of them. Let's stay on topic, and please stop interrupting me!"

Ashlynne's face burned from the rebuke, but she stayed silent for the rest of the explanation.

Mimi continued, "This type of Faerie has fangs but doesn't use them to bite its human victims. I don't know what they are used for, and it may simply be a glamoury that is used for effect. It has the hooves of a deer, and again, I don't know why that is. Baobhan Sith use their long fingernails to dig and scratch into the skin of humans then drink the blood that flows after the abrasion."

"Vamp-Fae," muttered Ashlynne.

"Yes, that about sums it up, Dear."

"Can they kill humans?"

"Oh, they most certainly can, should they choose to. If Bennette is here, then the one that killed me is here as well."

"Wait, what? What do you mean by the one that killed you? Mimi, you've never told me that you were killed by a Faerie!" Ashlynne shouted.

"Well, I suppose it never came up," the spirit replied as she lit a cigarette and blew smoke rings in a feeble attempt to remain calm.

Mimi was, truth be told, afraid for herself and for her young friend.

"Is that why you're feeling sick? Because this Faerie is here?" Ashlynne asked.

"I think so, yes. The Faerie killed my physical body, but my spirit still knows its energy and reacts to it the same way you would react to poison in a teacup. This Faerie is poisonous to me, Ashlynne."

"Oh, Mimi. What are we going to do?"

"You are going to narrow down those stones and find the Journey Stone that will free Meredith. I will think about how to handle the Baobhan Sith. Until then, it's best to assume that the coven knows everything about you. We know Bennette does. Now, whether Bennette has shared all his knowledge with the coven isn't certain, but I think it's safest to assume that he has."

"OK. Mimi?"

"Yes, Dear?"

"How does Bennette know about me?"

Mimi paused, "I'm afraid that's a very long tale for another time, Dear."

"Are you going to be OK?"

"Of course, Dear. I will be perfectly OK, no matter what."

Chapter 23

Ashlynne heaved the heavy pile of freshly washed towels into the dryer and set it to run on the longest cycle before returning to her kitchen area for a cup of much-needed coffee. Everything that Mimi had told her ran through her head in a tangle of words, definitions, feelings, and images until it was indecipherable. Coffee would help. Coffee always helped.

She sat at the old-fashioned oak dining table, chin in her hands, staring at the line of cupboards across the room. The glass-fronted doors showcased cake plates and stands, glass and plastic pitchers, and the largest variety of salt and pepper shakers she had ever seen collected in a private home.

As she stared at the cupboard and its shelves of entertainment accouterments, the conversation with Mimi loosened and untangled in her head, just enough to pull together a semblance of meaning.

"OK, first, Mimi died from a blood-drinking Faerie. Why didn't she tell us this before, Murphy? And why didn't I ask her before now how she died?" she asked the dog.

Murphy worked on the nylon bone that Ashlynne had ordered with the groceries, only twitching an ear in perfunctory response to his human's voice.

"Also, what the hell is it with a blood-drinking Faerie? Seriously, those Grimm brothers sure dropped the ball when re-telling old folklore. Fairy tales are all well and good but warning us about the type of creatures that actually drink our blood would have been more than helpful," she continued as she gulped the last of her coffee and stood to pour more from the carafe on the counter.

Returning to her chair with a fresh cup of her drug of choice, she continued to work out, piece by piece, the summer's events and the new information from Mimi.

"So, Faeries are back—check. This time it's a blood-drinking Faerie—check, check. And it's a blood-drinking Faerie that's attached to Witches—check, check, check. Witches have trapped one of their own inside a doll with a magic stone, and I am here to set her free— check, check, check, check," she recited, ticking off the salient points with her fingers.

"I wonder if the Faerie will leave once Meredith is free? Well, there's a thought, Murphy. Will Meredith kick the coven out of her house? I hope so, but I should ask Mimi how she feels about that."

Feeling more organized and caffeinated, Ashlynne scooped up Murphy and his bone and climbed the stairs to her suite.

"No matter what, Murphy, we need to find the correct Journey Stone. Hopefully, we can get that settled before setting out the coven's wine and cheese platters this evening."

Ashlynne deposited Murphy at the foot of the bed and found the hag stone she had brought from New Orleans. Using the last of the blue thread, she threaded the stone, doubling and tripling the thread so it was strong enough to hold the stone yet allowing it to swing freely.

"Good thing Michele taught us about scrying," she remarked to Murphy who watched with interest.

Happy with the weight and swing of her improvised pendulum, Ashlynne grabbed a handful of stones from the large basket and held the hag stone suspended over each one, waiting to see if the stone moved or reacted in any way to an enchantment.

Stone after stone, the pendulum hung

mute and still. Slowly, the pile in the basket reduced in size as the discarded pile of tested stones grew larger. The light outside her windows mellowed, signifying that the afternoon was rapidly coming to a close.

"Ugh! Murphy, this looks impossible!" groaned Ashlynne as she stood and stretched, feeling joints and muscles pop and creak after sitting on the floor for so long.

"OK, potty break for me and some water, and then we'll test a few more stones before I have to go do the work I'm being paid for," she said to the dog.

She returned to her room, now scattered with hundreds of Journey Stones, and surveyed the mess. It seemed impossible to locate the one enchanted stone amongst the hundreds of decoys.

"There has got to be a better way than this," she muttered, "Enchantments are spells and spells are energy, right, Murphy? Then let's try finding this needle in the haystack my own way—sorry, Michele", she added with a smile to her much-missed friend.

Planting both feet firmly on the hardwood floor and dropping her arms to her sides, Ashlynne breathed deeply, in through her mouth and out through her nose until she felt grounded and strong. Holding her right arm out, palm open and aimed at the piles of stones, she breathed as she moved her consciousness out to the stones scattered across the floor. Wisps of images and memories held within the minerals drifted past her as she explored the different piles. A lonely man walking the beach picked up the green granite stone with the pink band running around its circumference to study it.

Finding it interesting but not interesting enough to take home, he dropped it back into the sand. A seagull pushed the gray-colored stone away from the candy wrapper still holding a bit of chocolate, unaware and uncaring that the white ribbon of quartz banding the sandstone made it anything special at all. Ashlynne allowed the whispers to float past her and waited for the tingle and shimmer of colors that would alert her to a spell.

After a while, her arm felt sore and she raised it over her head, swinging it in a large circle to loosen the bunched muscles. On the third swing, with her hand behind her, she saw a smudge of dark red shot through with dull silver—the same energy that had played out around the last full moon, and the same energy that had pushed her back when she investigated the disturbing omen.

"Ahhh, this is you. Isn't it, Stella?" whispered Ashlynne as she turned her body to feel more closely the impression from the stone that sent out the energy of the enchantment.

Her palm tingled and itched, a slightly painful sensation, as the full power of the spell revealed itself. The angry energy, pulsing red and silver, enveloped her hand and snaked up her arm. Ashlynne resumed her careful breathing technique to quell her rising panic as Stella's spell wrapped itself up and around her forearm.

Feeling grounded again, Ashlynne shook her arm sharply, sending the red miasma into the floor, and opened her eyes. The stone that was filled with the spell's energy was a dark green granite, roughly egg-shaped, with a distinctive, unbroken band—a shimmering bright white strip of crystalline quartz. Holding it in her hand, she could feel the zip and pop of the powerful spell completely at odds with the nondescript beach stone.

"Gotcha," she muttered as she wrapped her hard-won prize in a velvet glove she had found in the bottom drawer of her dresser when she first arrived. The velvet was old and heavy, and the color and fabric were a solid black, perfect for protecting and muting the power of the stone.

Stashing the stone under the mounds of pillows on her bed for the time being, she gathered the rest, piled them into the basket, and repeated the incantation to safely exit the protective circle. She hoisted the heavy basket of assorted Journey Stones onto one hip and walked purposely across the landing to Stella's door. As she entered without knocking, a tight smile of anger and indignation spread across her face. She dropped the wicker basket with a furious bounce back onto the bed where she had originally found it.

"Check mate," she said grimly as she started down the back stairwell to prepare the evening wine and cheese sampling, Murphy trailing behind her.

Ashlynne was so intent on sending a message to Stella that she had recited the spell that opened the protective circle around her suite but forgot to close it after she left. The space was left open and available for anyone who wanted to enter.

The Faerie, the Baobhan Sith, felt a shimmer as the circle was taken down, and by now she was used to this. She knew that the Witch, Stella, wanted desperately to get into the young woman's suite, and if the Witch desired it, the Faerie was aware. Expecting the next shimmer of energy to signify that the circle had closed, the Faerie grinned in delight when it never occurred.

Moving to the landing to investigate, the blood-drinker felt a familiar tug and pull; a human it had fed on was inside the suite. How could that be? There was no one here but the Witch who it had feasted from before. The Faerie was certain of this. However, the pull was unmistakable and oh so delightful.

The Faerie slipped into Ashlynne's suite and sniffed the air, its cloven deer's feet clip-clopping on the hardwood flooring. Meredith shrank further into the doll, aware of the new presence. Pushing the door open to the sitting room, the Baobhan Sith's mouth pulled back in a fearsome smile, its sharp teeth gleaming. The ornate mirror on its footed frame glowed and sparked in the gathering twilight of the evening, a harbinger of the fireworks that would begin later when the sun had fully set.

On another floor of Rosehaven, Bennette sat as still as a statue, feeling the waves of movement pulse and flow throughout the massive house—the shrinking of Meredith as she moved further into her prison, the grim amusement of the young redhead who had found the enchanted stone, and the murderous glee of the Faerie who had discovered an old foe.

As the voices of the Witches chattered, moving down to the dining room for the nightly ritual of wine, cheese, and plotting, Bennette feared that a very long night lay ahead.

Ashlynne finished servicing the guests' rooms, a task she had become both efficient and proficient at. The regular housekeepers had been given this week off to enjoy the Venetian festivities with their families.

While it may have appeared benevolent and generous for her to have done so, Ashlynne's motives were purely selfish—she needed all extra workers clear of the house while she prepared for the release of Meredith. The final groceries had been ordered and delivered, all breakfast pastries had been picked up from the bakery and stored in the lower catering kitchen, the floral arrangements had been freshened by the florist, and the gardeners finished their work a few days ago.

Ashlynne started the laundry and climbed the stairs to the main kitchen to clean up the breakfast debris. She no longer resented playing maid to a group of people that would gladly do her harm, but she was on full alert now.

She listened to conversations and social plans and observed every step that the group made so that she could make her own plans to free Meredith.

While the Venetian Festival technically began earlier in the week, tonight marked the final grand weekend with elaborate fireworks, a lighted boat parade in the yacht basin at Round Lake, a carnival with a massive Ferris wheel in the middle of downtown, and vending trucks of all descriptions parked along Bridge Street which would be closed to traffic for the duration of the weekend.

It would be a small-town version of Mardi Gras, and Ashlynne was planning for the upheaval and madness to distract the others from her plans at Rosehaven.

Snagging a raspberry Danish from the platter of breakfast pastries, Ashlynne closed the window blinds against the gathering late-

July heat and went upstairs to her suite to shower and get dressed.

Murphy lounged in front of the tall mirror in the sitting room with his nylon bone resting between his front paws. He watched the scene play out within the mirror's ornate frame. He heard the shower running and Ashlynne singing loudly, so he knew he had a little bit of time before she was out of the bathroom. He watched as the images gathered together then floated away like fog—the large owl with no scent was flying low over the city of Charlevoix providing a literal bird's-eye view of the small town bursting at the seams with carnival rides, tourists, locals, boats, and food trucks.

As Murphy watched, the scene broke up and floated away, replaced by the back garden where robed figures stood encircling a dark-haired woman and the green-skinned monster. As the scene drew in, Murphy assumed he was, again, watching from the owl's perspective. The monster made long scratches on the dark-haired lady's neck then leaned in and lapped up the blood it had drawn delicately, like a cat.

Murphy whined as the monster looked up, appearing to look directly at him. He was more familiar with monsters than he would like to be and wasn't happy to see that he and his human had arrived in the domain of yet another one. That scene broke and floated away, and Murphy was glad. While he knew that the green-skinned thing couldn't truly see him, it had left him feeling shaky.

His key-shaped scar burned and itched in response. As he waited to see what picture would show up in the mirror next, Murphy wondered if he would see Papa Legba again. While he was a little frightening, Murphy knew him to be good and strong, and it would be comforting to have him back with them.

"Hello, Murphy," greeted Mimi as she sat in her familiar chair.

While he was drifting within his own memories, Mimi had arrived in the mirror's glass. Murphy wiggled and wagged in response to the spirit's raspy voice and sat up in his prettiest pose.

"You are a good boy, Murphy—the best boy!" smiled Mimi as the small but feisty terrier leaned forward to hear what she had to say.

"You've seen the Faerie with the Witches, yes? And Meredith's owl has shown you the crowds in the city for this weekend."

Murphy whined and lowered his head. He wanted nothing to do with the thing in the Witches' circle.

"I know. The Faerie is quite frightening, but you won't need to bother with it. I just wanted you to know that it is here, and it knows about us. What I need you to do is to keep Ashlynne on track to release Meredith from the doll. I will deal with the Baobhan Sith because, in truth, I should have done that long ago. I left my story unfinished, and it's time now for me to write the final chapter, as it were. But you and Ashlynne are far from any final anything's, and I want to make sure of that! So, your job is to keep her away from the monster and help her set Meredith free. Meredith and her owl will not only protect her but finish this mess so you may both return home safely. Are we clear, Murphy?"

Murphy whined in agreement and watched as the mirror filled with thick cigarette smoke, completely obscuring Mimi from view. The glass just started to clear when he heard the shower turn off. Giving the mirror one last look and seeing nothing there save for the reflection of the room, he took his bone and crossed into the bedroom where he scootched under the bed to gnaw on the information he got from the mirror as well as his bone.

Ashlynne dried herself off and wound her long hair up into the towel as she gathered her clothes for the day. It was early, just after nine, but it would be warm soon. She chose a pair of shorts, a t-shirt with a New Orleans creole cottage printed on the front, and her tennis shoes.

As much as she would have preferred flip-flops, the sound that they made as she ran up and down the stairs at Rosehaven grated on her nerves. Slipping her arms into a lightweight cotton sweater, she smeared sunblock onto her face and shook her hair out to let it air dry as she made her bed and wiped down her bathroom.

After she completed what she considered her adult chores, Ashlynn sat down at the small wicker desk in her bedroom to make notes and decide on her new plan of attack.

After speaking at length with Mimi, they had decided that deception was their best bet for releasing Meredith from the doll before the Witches and Stella knew what was happening.

Checking the city's event calendar on her phone, she saw that the night's activities would begin at seven with the first of three outdoor concerts followed by the voting for the Venetian Queen and her court. To end the evening, the fireworks display would commence over Lake Michigan. Tomorrow night would be more of the same, only swapping out the Venetian Queen votes for the boat parade, but Ashlynne wanted to begin her plan tonight.

If for some reason tonight failed, she would—hopefully—have a second chance to free Meredith on Saturday night. It was important to make her first attempt tonight. The built-in chaos of the festival and the immense amount of energy that would be flowing around the town would make for a good distraction; Ashlynne's work could hide behind it, obscured from the Witches better than if she tried to free Meredith on some random weekend in August. Or so she hoped.

She took the enchanted Journey Stone from its hiding place and removed it from the velvet opera glove. She slipped it into a small drawstring satin bag that originally held jewelry, but the bag now held the extra beach stones that she had collected at the beginning of her stay. She cinched the small bag closed and hid it in the very bottom drawer of her dresser hoping that the energy of the other beach stones would mute the enchantment of the Journey Stone should anyone come looking for it.

A decoy stone was placed into a small paper bag, the type with handles that nice gift shops handed out. The paper gift bag had the name of a local women's and children's clothing store embossed on the front so it wouldn't look out of place as she walked through downtown later. The bag would, however, pique the interest of Camryn who seemed to be the assigned lookout for everything that Ashlynne did, and that is exactly what Ashlynne and Mimi hoped would continue.

"Murphy! Where did you go?" she called to the dog who had not made an appearance since before her shower.

As Ashlynne gathered the decoy stone and Murphy's leash, the small dog emerged from under the bed and yawned loudly.

"I know, it's been an exhausting few weeks, Murph. Hopefully, this will all be over in a day or two. Let's leave this bag for Camryn to snoop around in while you and I go for a walk, OK?"

She clipped the leash and harness into place and slung the bag's handles over her wrist as she said the words that allowed her to exit her suite through the magic circle that she had set up so many weeks ago. On the landing, she repeated the process and ran down the back stairwell to leave the bag on the dining room table where it couldn't help but be seen.

Unfortunately, Ashlynne hadn't realized that she had neglected to properly close the magic circle previously—a mistake that left the regulated opening and closing completely discombobulated now, and the circle of protection surrounding her room was shredded.

While Ashlynne was unaware of her misstep, Meredith and Bennette were not. Meredith sent her own powerful magics out from the doll that imprisoned her to secure the closet where she was kept. She would have preferred to secure the girl's space as well, but she didn't have her full range of strength. Meredith was comforted knowing that at least her owl was keeping tabs on the girl and the dog through the spirit, Mimi.

Bennette was not concerned with the imprisoned Witch. Meredith's release had nothing to do with his purpose at Rosehaven. It was the fact that the Baobhan Sith could now enter the girl's suite that made him take notice. Long ago, something had begun that had remained unfinished; his job was to see that it was finally completed.

Chapter 25

Camryn stepped quickly down the grand staircase and turned into the dining room on her way to the kitchen. The others were still in their rooms and though breakfast was over, she was still hungry. She was looking forward to a pastry and another cup of coffee without Stella's lectures, rantings, and accusations that came every time the group was together.

In truth, Camryn felt that the coven's cohesiveness was beginning to fray and thought that Stella did as well. With their manufactured enemy secured in the doll, the purpose of the coven was now limited to destroying the doll—and hopefully Meredith with it—and gathering in ritual to feed the

Faerie that Stella insisted gave her great power. Camryn had her own ideas about who was granting power to whom but kept those to herself for now.

Deep in thought on the state of the coven, Camryn was two steps past the dining room table before the gift bag registered in her mind. Turning back, she peeked inside the bag then stared thoughtfully out the French doors at the garden beyond. The Journey Stone was in the bag. Stella had already called the coven together to let them know that Ashlynne had found the stone; could she have been so dumb as to leave it here? She smiled ruefully. She was right in thinking that the House Manager was no one to be concerned about. Even if the girl did have the abilities that Stella insisted that she did, she wasn't terribly bright—something that Cam had suspected all along.

Camryn snagged the small bag and carried it into the kitchen. She poured a cup of coffee and nibbled thoughtfully on a Danish as she considered her options. She could leave the bag where she had found it and let another member of the group deal with the discovery, she could bring the bag to Stella providing herself with another figurative gold star from the High Priestess, or she could take matters into her own hands.

Cam stuffed the half-eaten pastry down the garbage disposal, dumped her coffee in after it, and left her coffee cup in the sink. She made her decision.

"No time like the present, huh, Lady?" she said quietly to herself as she grabbed the bag and left Rosehaven. This small step would bring her closer to the position within the group that she had always known would be hers.

The July morning sunshine cast bright polka dots on the sidewalk as Camryn walked swiftly toward the drawbridge and the downtown area. Even this early in the day the small city center was teeming with tourists and visitors wandering through the art fair tents, grabbing coffee from the food vendors, or feeding the trout in the fishponds in the lakeside parks.

Taking notice but not caring, Camryn turned right onto Park Avenue and walked briskly past the large clapboard homes with their shaded wrap-around porches and peaked roofs. Large and traditionally midwestern, these homes were nothing like the mansions on Michigan Avenue to the north. As she walked further down the pretty street closer to Lake Michigan, the homes were larger and slightly grander but still not as fancy as Rosehaven, her home for the summer—it was a thought that made her grin.

"Ah, there you are," she said under her breath as she approached a steep hill to her right that sloped down to a small beachside park on the shores of Lake Michigan. Jutting out from the pier that ran along Pine River Channel was Charlevoix's iconic red lighthouse. Camryn was glad to see that the area was empty except for a few men fishing along the railings.

Passing the stone beach wall separating the sand from the sidewalk on her left and the large DNR Fisheries building to her right, Camryn ambled along the pier swinging the small bag casually; just a lone tourist out for a mid-morning stroll. She smiled at the bored older man holding a fishing pole and approached the end of the pier. Lake Michigan stretched endlessly on, an inland ocean of immense power.

Camryn stood for a minute, breathing in the fresh air that rolled off the cold waters, and removed the Journey Stone from the gift bag. She threw the stone as far into the lake as she was able. It hit the blue water with a plunk and dropped into the water's depths.

"And that is that. Meredith can stay put in

the damn doll if we can't find it, and we can finish our stay and be gone in a few weeks. I've had enough of this cloak and dagger crap. I think the others have too. It may be time for a change in leadership when the summer is done," she said with a grim yet determined grin on her face.

She turned and walked back down the pier past the bored old man and his thousand-yard stare. She never noticed the large owl that sat silent and watchful on the ledge of the lighthouse, nor did its shadow as it flew over her head alert her to anything amiss. As far as Camryn was concerned, she had just instigated a subtle yet soon-to-be-effective coup.

The owl watched as the woman threw the decoy stone into the lake and took off to report the information to its Mistress and the spirit in the mirror. While it was unclear to the familiar if this was what the redhead had planned, it suspected that this turn of events was a positive one. The massive bird cruised north into a gathering cloud bank, winking out of sight.

Imprisoned within the doll, yet safe for now, Meredith closed her eyes at the call of her familiar and watched the scene that it sent her way. The Witch smiled and sent a silent smile of gratitude to Ashlynne; it seemed that there might be hope for her freedom after all.

Chapter 26

Ashlynne sat cross-legged in the stuffy sitting room and watched the images in the mirror like a personal movie screen. There was no air conditioning in this room and no breeze outside. The heat gathered from downstairs and settled here which was why she spent very little time in this room, as charming as it was. However, when she and Murphy returned from their walk and noticed the gift bag was missing from the dining room table, Ashlynne thought it best to check with Mimi before she proceeded. She was worried that one of the housekeepers had returned to check on the house, found the bag, and disposed of it.

She sipped her water and watched, through the mirror, as Camryn chose to throw the decoy stone into the lake rather than inform the coven or Stella—a development that Ashlynne found both surprising and delightful since it left Stella none the wiser and Camryn with the idea that the real Journey Stone was gone.

"This is a happy turn of events, isn't it, Murphy?" said Ashlynne to the small dog who was busy crunching ice cubes from a bowl she had brought upstairs with them.

"We can thank Meredith and her owl for the visual account of this," said Mimi, stepping into the frame as the last images of Camryn dissipated like fog.

"Yes, that is amazingly convenient, isn't it?" asked Ashlynne with the slightest hint of sarcasm in her voice, "However did that come to be?"

"Oh, stop, Ashlynne. I already said I was sorry to have brought you here," snapped

Mimi, lighting her Chesterfield King and inhaling deeply.

"I would still like to know."

"Well, the details are a little out of your realm, Dear—literally. But suffice it to say that when Meredith wound up in her, um, predicament, she sent her owl out to look for help. The owl found me, I thought of you, and here we are!" chirped the normally sardonic spirit with an exaggerated shrug of her shoulders and a ridiculously upbeat tone of voice.

Ashlynne narrowed her eyes at Mimi, "Yes. Here we are."

"Please don't be upset, Dear. I honestly had no idea that this would get so out of hand or that another Faerie would be here. You needed a job and Meredith needed help. I thought it would be a simple matter for someone with your talents."

"It's OK, Mimi. We're getting closer to resolving the situation now, I think," replied

Ashlynne with genuine warmth.

She hated to see her friend feeling so guilty. Truth be told, Ashlynne would have come here even if she had known the whole truth of the matter because she also believed that she had the skills to release Meredith. It was Mimi's well-being that concerned her the most now.

Finishing their meeting, Mimi wandered off to wherever she wandered off to, and Ashlynne and Murphy exited the sitting room in exchange for the cool lake breezes that were available in the bedroom.

"We have a couple of hours before the coven goes downtown for the festival, Murphy. How about a quick snooze so we're ready for the evening?" Ashlynne asked the dog as she kicked off her tennis shoes and curled up on the bed with a light blanket draped over her legs.

Murphy joined her, winding himself around her hip and matching his breathing with hers.

Ashlynne struggled to open her eyes as she kept getting pulled back into the dream; a beautiful woman was walking toward her with dark brown hair caught back at her neck with a silver filigree comb. She was dressed in a dark green velvet gown with an artfully fitted bodice that showed the swell of her breasts. A small smile played on her lips. The sound of her footsteps on the bedroom's hardwood floors was loud and striking.

Ashlynne thought groggily that the woman must be wearing heels. She tried desperately to wake up. There was nothing unpleasant about the dream yet the feeling of being caught like prey was overwhelming and terrifying.

Clip-clop, clip-clop, the woman walked closer to the bed as Ashlynne struggled to get up. The closer the woman approached, the less attractive she became. Her skin began to crinkle like used tissue and turned from the perfect porcelain it had first shown to the gray-green color of mold.

"This can't be," moaned Ashlynne.

The resemblance to the Faerie Morag was unmistakable.

Clip-clop, clip-clop, closer and closer came the Faerie. Ashlynne was able to move her head to see what shoes this thing was wearing that made such a loud and unusual sound.

"Oh my god," she moaned in a rush of exhaled breath.

Not shoes. Not shoes at all. The Faerie's feet were deer hooves, and each step rang out on the floorboards like the mules' hooves that pulled the tour carriages in the French Quarter.

The Faerie moved closer, and its appearance grew more terrifying; its lips were grotesquely engorged and red with long sharp fangs protruding from within its mouth. As Ashlynne lay still—completely unable to move now—the Faerie lifted its hand. Fingers ending in dagger-like fingernails reached for her neck. Desperately trying to get the scream out that was stuck in her throat, Ashlynne could only watch as the Faerie crooked its index finger, preparing to gouge her skin and release beads of blood for a snack.

A blur of movement took Ashlynne by such surprise that she was able to sit up in time to see that Murphy had launched himself off the bed and was spinning madly in circles snapping and growling at nothing but air.

"Murph! Murphy! It's OK! It's gone now!" cried Ashlynne as she picked up the writhing bundle of fur and held it close.

"I don't think it was here, Murphy, not really here. I also don't think that was just a dream, I mean, unless we're sharing dreams now," she whispered to the small dog that rested limply in her arms.

"I guess my magic circle wasn't able to keep a Faerie out," whispered Ashlynne as she looked around the room, half expecting to see the fanged, cloven-hoofed creature hiding in the shadows.

Murphy continued to grumble and growl, his heart racing painfully in his small chest. He knew that Ashlynne's circle had been horribly compromised but hadn't been able to get her to check for its energy or pay enough attention when going in and out to fix it.

He supposed his human had a lot on her mind, but he was frustrated that she had let something so important lapse so horribly. He decided that from now until they could get out of here, he would sleep under the bed where he could see what and who came into the bedroom before Ashlynne was in too much danger.

Ashlynne set the dog down and took a long swallow of her water. She felt overwhelmed and scared, and she was unsure about which dangerous situation she should tackle first—the Vampire-Faerie or the trapped Witch. As she watched the seagulls spin and whirl on the currents over the lake, she decided that she would proceed as planned by releasing Meredith first. Then, if necessary, she would figure out how to deal with the Faerie. Hopefully, Mimi would have some ideas about that when the time came.

The sunlight had turned a deep, mellow gold as the day moved on toward evening, and Ashlynne's stomach growled to remind her that she had yet to feed herself or the dog.

"First things first, Murphy. We should never battle Faeries and release imprisoned Witches on empty stomachs. Let's go find some dinner."

She muttered the incantation to allow her out and opened the door for Murphy. After Murphy was out, she followed him through, closed the door, and said the appropriate words to reset the circle—though she doubted this was effective any longer.

Ashlynne followed the dog down the three

flights of stairs to the small catering kitchen and fixed him his usual pumpkin and kibble. She was hungry but not in the mood to cook, so she made a plate for herself of cheese wedges, grapes, smoked fish from the local fish market, crackers, and some salted cashews. She absentmindedly stuck bits of food into her mouth and chewed without tasting as she mentally went over what she needed to do after the coven leaves later this evening.

It would not be too complicated so long as she had the house to herself for a little while. By the sounds of the excited voices in the kitchen above her, it seemed that she would. She could hear as they made plans for a dinner out, cocktails on the Weathervane's balcony, and watching the concerts in the park; all in all, it would be a full evening of festival activities.

"Good," she muttered around a grape and took a drink of some lemonade, "I need to get this show on the road and get back home. I've had just about enough small-town fun and games. How about you, Murphy?"

Murphy barked once, spun in a circle, and sat as pretty as possible; he was absolutely ready to go home.

Chapter 27

Ashlynne heard the large double doors slam shut as the coven left the house and clattered down the front porch steps. She looked out the windows at the top of the main staircase's landing on the second floor to see the group sauntering down the sidewalk to join other groups, some larger and some smaller, all headed to Bridge Street to enjoy the last big weekend of Venetian Festival.

"OK, Murphy—it's showtime!" declared Ashlynne as she raced to the door of her suite and threw it open, no longer bothering with magic circles or incantations.

Murphy jumped onto the bed and watched as Ashlynne extracted the bag of beach stones with the enchanted Journey Stone from the dresser drawer and then retrieved the doll in its small trunk from the closet.

"I'm nervous, Murphy. What if I don't do this right or hurt Meredith?" Ashlynne closed her eyes and took a deep breath, "No time like the present, Ash," she said under her breath and unclasped the brass lock that held the trunk closed.

The doll lay safely within, its elaborate Victorian dress hardly creased, and the painted face the picture of serenity. Ashlynne carefully lifted the large figure and placed it on the floor. She wasn't sure how Meredith would exit the doll, and she didn't want to rescue the Witch only to have her fall off the dresser and break an ankle.

"OK, here we go!" Ashlynne announced.

Ashlynne retrieved the Journey Stone from the small bag and held it loosely in her left hand. Planting her feet firmly on the floor and wiggling her toes, she took three deep breaths and closed her eyes. She heard Murphy make low rumbling noises as the lamps and overhead lights throughout Rosehaven flickered off and on—a precursor of the fireworks scheduled for later that evening.

"Eliza! It's OK!" Ashlynne called.

Not only could she see the lights blinking behind her closed eyelids, but she could feel the spirit spinning in a typhoon of anxiety, or was it excitement?

"Settle down, Eliza! I need to get this done before they all come back!" hissed Ashlynne as the lamps continued their erratic light show.

Trying her best to ignore the dog's growling and the ghost's display of emotion, Ashlynne settled her feet once again on the floor, breathed in deeply, then exhaled to release her nervousness. At the third breath, she felt strong and calm and opened her eyes.

The doll lay where she had placed it, but now Ashlynne could see the spinning dark red energy pulsing with a dull silver that surrounded the effigy. Stella's enchantment was perfectly visible to her now. She held her right hand out, palm open to the doll, and concentrated on the energy within it.

For the first time, Ashlynne could see an image of the woman that she had been tasked to free. Dark blond hair the color of honey framed a heart-shaped face with piercing green eyes. While pretty, there was a hardness to Meredith that seemed to be at odds with her classic features. Her energy was dark green with notes of sparkling teal, the colors of the waves that crashed below the cliffs of Rosehaven. For all of Stella's fire, Meredith's calm water hid the fathomless depths and quiet strength that could be cold as ice and underestimated at one's peril. It seemed that Stella had made that mistake, and Ashlynne cringed to think of the price that she would pay for it.

Steeling herself against the Witch's

strength, Ashlynne pulled the dark green energy away from the doll. Concentrating on the center of the Witch's chest, Ashlynne breathed in deeply and pulled at the same time, gritting her teeth against the spell that Stella had cast.

"Come ON, Meredith! Work with me!" she spat through clenched teeth as she slowly extracted the essence of Meredith from her porcelain prison.

All the while, the lamps and lights in Rosehaven continued to flicker on and off madly with no central rhythm — a kaleidoscope of electricity that made Ashlynne feel dizzy and fatigued.

"This isn't working, Meredith! I can't get you out!" cried Ashlynne to the specter of the Witch.

Gritting her teeth and bending her knees for one more monumental pull, Ashlynne swung her left hand over her head, adding it to her energy that would hopefully release

Meredith.

The lights all went out. Ashlynne felt a pop and ducked, expecting a shower of glass from the chandelier above her head. But it wasn't the light bulbs that had made the sound—it was the Journey Stone breaking in half. She dropped the pieces and groped around on her dresser to find her lighter for visibility. As the flickering flame illuminated the room, Ashlynne jumped back with a yelp—she wasn't alone any longer.

"Oh! It worked!" she cried as Meredith steadied herself against the dresser, weak from being trapped for so long.

"Murphy! It worked! We did it!" she laughed as she grabbed the still grumbling dog and danced him in circles.

"Hello, Ashlynne," smiled Meredith in a surprisingly deep voice, "Thank you so much for getting me out of there. I owe you and Eliza an enormous debt."

"Eliza? Why Eliza?" asked Ashlynne, her

head spinning.

"When Stella used the Journey Stone to move me from this world into the world within the doll, she upset the natural balance of things. You've heard the adage 'nature abhors a vacuum?'" Meredith asked.

"Yes," whispered Ashlynne.

"Well, it's absolutely true. Nature will automatically establish balance in the easiest way possible. It's a fundamental law. When I was removed from this plane, it left a hole—a space that was supposed to be filled here at Rosehaven. To fill that hole, Eliza was brought in."

"Hadn't Eliza always been here?" asked Ashlynne.

"Yes and no. This was Eliza's home a long time ago, and she loved Rosehaven very much. Small parts of her remained, little bits of her energy just like bits of you remain in places that you love, even after you've left. Think of them as memories. But when a hole emerged where I was supposed to be, the natural law sought to fill it in the most efficient way possible, and that was to bring all of Eliza back here. She became just as much a prisoner of Stella's magic as I was," Meredith explained.

"But if she loved it here…"

Meredith interrupted, "Because she had already died and moved to her afterlife to rest. That rest was taken from her. While she loved her former home, she didn't want to be stuck within it, unable to leave or rest. Do you understand now?"

"I think so, yes. Thank you for explaining. What will you do about Stella and the others?"

"Oh, I have interesting plans for them, don't you worry about that group at all."

While Meredith smiled, it was so full of anger and malice that Ashlynne was glad that she wasn't part of Stella's coven; crossing Meredith could be deadly.

"Where is Eliza now, Meredith?"

"She has been released from Rosehaven and returned to her place of rest until, or if, she decides to come back to this plane of existence.

"Is that how death works then? We rest and can return if we want?" Ashlynne asked.

"Sometimes, yes. And sometimes, no."

Ashlynne left it at that, not wanting to ask too many questions at once and understanding that she would not receive another answer about that topic from Meredith.

Meredith, Ashlynne, and Murphy made their way down to the kitchen as the festival's fireworks shot up and exploded overhead, making colors dance on the damask wall coverings and splash across the wool rugs of the main floor.

In Meredith's weakened state she was

unable to separate the feel of Stella's energy in the house from the Faerie's energy.

She was unaware when the Baobhan Sith quietly stole away into Ashlynne's suite in search of the spirit that it had once known.

Chapter 28

As the moon rose high over Rosehaven, visible now with the completion of the fireworks display, Ashlynne and Meredith sat silently—and at times uncomfortably—in the large kitchen nursing a bottle of wine and their thoughts. Ashlynne watched Meredith over the rim of her wine glass and could not begin to fathom what the other woman felt. There was no spark of colored energy, no random images of her thoughts, nothing at all. Meredith was closed like a vault, and Ashlynne wasn't sure whether to be irritated or in awe.

"When do you think they'll come back here?" asked Ashlynne, breaking the heavy silence.

"They won't," replied Meredith with a disturbing finality.

Ashlynne wanted to know more, so much more! But the hard-set nature of Meredith's features warned her that more questions were unwelcome.

"I'll be right back. I forgot my phone in my room," said Ashlynne as she downed the last of her wine and pushed her chair back from the table.

Seeing no response one way or the other from the Witch, and assuming she was free to go, Ashlynne walked briskly through the butler's pantry and turned to walk up the service stairs to the second floor. Her heart clenched as she realized that there would be no more flickering lights or lamps left on; she was going to miss Eliza.

As she reached the landing, Murphy shot up in front of her, barking and growling at the open door and scaring her half to death.

"Murphy! What the hell is wrong with you?" snapped Ashlynne.

It was an uncharacteristically angry response. She was rarely short-tempered with her canine companion, but she was beyond exhausted at this point and had no patience for his overprotective antics.

Murphy refused to move and, small as he was, he was blocking the entrance to her room and making a terrible racket.

"Stop it, Murph. Stop it right now!" demanded Ashlynne as she quickly grabbed the terrier from the back to avoid his snapping teeth and dropped him behind her.

While she doubted he would ever purposely bite her, she could see that he was agitated and didn't want him to accidentally draw blood.

"I think we've all had enough of Rosehaven's fun and games—you included," she said, giving him a stern side-eye that left Murphy with his head down in both defeat and shame. Nonetheless, he continued to grumble and growl his concerns at the back of his throat, all of which Ashlynne chose to ignore.

"We're done, Murphy. We've completed what we were brought here for, and we don't need to ward or magic the rooms anymore. It's all good. I promise," she said over her shoulder as she walked into the darkened suite that had become her home away from home.

The moon shone through the French doors, washing the bedroom in a sultry, summer purple light reminding her of New Orleans. As she moved assorted hair ties, her brush, a single sock, and a book around on the dresser top searching for her phone, she heard a sound that made the hairs stand up on her neck and let her know in no uncertain terms that she had misjudged Murphy's temper tantrum.

Clip-clop. Clip-clop. Clip-clop.

Ashlynne moaned and Murphy growled. The Faerie stopped moving.

"Murphy, let's go," whispered Ashlynne as she carefully turned toward the bedroom door. Murphy had stopped his growls and understood that the need for silence outweighed the need for a warning.

The Faerie stood in the small hallway between Ashlynne's bedroom and the sitting room, blocking her exit to the second-floor landing. The moonlight didn't reach that far into the suite, but the creature's darkened silhouette was unmistakable.

Clip-clop. Clip-clop.

The Baobhan Sith moved into the bedroom, its bright green eyes shining in the purple moonlight leaving Ashlynne terrified and immobile. She was prey, and she knew it. Murphy, however, was not rendered still or silent and rushed at the monster who responded with a swift kick to the small dog with its sharp, hoofed foot. With a yelp,

Murphy dropped and remained there, a small furry lump in the moonlit room.

Ashlynne tried to cry out but no sound could escape, and her eyes rolled in her head as the vampiric being moved in, wrapping its arms around her and bending her neck like a lover's, nails extended like daggers.

As the razor-sharp fingernails raked the sensitive skin of her neck, first a light tickle moving into a deep burn, Ashlynne closed her eyes in resignation.

As she floated away in a mental fog born of terror and the hypnotic magic from the Baobhan Sith, Ashlynne was yanked back to the present by an incredible flash of golden brilliance that sparked from behind her closed eyes. Blinking rapidly to clear her vision in the dazzling light that illuminated the room like a bonfire, Ashlynne's mouth dropped open in surprise—standing in the white-hot center of the golden halo was Mimi.

Resplendent in her navy blue 1940's power

suit and spectator pumps, hair rolled to perfection, she stood with both hands on her hips—the very picture of feminine strength during her time on earth.

Many things happened at once, seen as rapid-fire pictures by Ashlynne. The Faerie—surprised as she was—dropped her, and she landed with a thud onto the hardwood next to the inert form of her dog.

"You will NOT!" she heard Mimi command as the Faerie rounded on her.

Mimi's deep and powerful command caused the fanged Faerie to hesitate. It was not expecting the power that came from the one it had once fed on to the point of death.

"I will do as I please as I have always done," hissed the Baobhan Sith through its fangs as its pillowed red lips spread in amusement, "Who are you to command me?"

"You will not take the girl. She is not for you," growled Mimi.

"You had your chance, but you retreated

into death, Miriam Blanchard. You have no recourse now. The human is mine to take or not as I choose."

"You're wrong. There was no retreat, simply a rest," Mimi said.

The Faerie laughed and turned back to Ashlynne who cringed against the edge of the bed in terror. She was not prepared for this being and had no idea how to protect herself against it.

Suddenly, golden brilliance enfolded the Faerie who responded as if burned. Shrieking and yelling as if it were being flayed alive, the creature writhed and struggled but it was of no use, Mimi held it fast and was dragging it through the bedroom door to the mirror in the sitting room.

Ashlynne grit her teeth against the combined assault of screeching from the Faerie and the scratching of its hooves on the hardwood floors.

As Mimi reached the mirror, she looked

beyond the struggling monster in her grip and smiled warmly at Ashlynne, "Goodbye, my Dear. It has been my honor and pleasure to have called you my friend. Please don't forget to bring a sweater when you go out."

Mimi fell backward into the mirror, bringing the Baobhan Sith and the golden brilliance with her.

"No! NO—Mimi! Come back! Don't leave me!" cried Ashlynne as she launched herself out of her bedroom and hit the mirror with a thud. But the mirror was only a mirror and did only what mirrors do; it reflected what was in front of it. In this case, the image in the glass was of a heartbroken young woman beating on the mirror's glass as the small terrier whose job it was to keep her safe sat behind her, sore but essentially uninjured.

"You can't go. You just can't," wept Ashlynne as she gathered Murphy onto her lap.

A voice interrupted her, "Miriam went

into the All, Ashlynne. It is the place that gathers us back into itself until it dreams of us anew."

Ashlynne jumped at the unknown voice that sounded behind her.

"Bennette!" she cried, her tears momentarily dried from the surprise, "Why are you here? How do you know Mimi?"

"I've known Miriam for a very long time, Ashlynne. Her story and mine are centuries in the making, and maybe I will share them with you at another time. For now, please know that what Miriam did was done for love," Bennette assured her.

"But why did she have to go? Why couldn't she have stayed in the mirror?" demanded Ashlynne.

"Her place in the mirror has always been temporary. She knew this."

Ashlynne buried her face in Murphy's warm body, absorbing all the comfort she could from her friend. When she had cried herself out of tears, feeling like a brittle corn husk, she looked up to find that Bennette was gone and the mirror remained just a mirror.

Ashlynne stood and scooped Murphy up carefully and returned to her bedroom. She gently placed the small dog on the bed, climbed in after him, and watched as Lake Michigan blew the trees this way and that. Try as she might, though, she couldn't see any smoke rings, and she thought that she would probably never stop looking for them.

Chapter 29

The next morning, Ashlynne stripped off the rumpled clothes that she had fallen asleep in and took a shower as hot as she could stand, scrubbing and washing away the horrors of the last few days. Her eyes were red and swollen from crying herself to sleep, something that no hot shower could fix.

Murphy had turned into a furry strip of Velcro, and she thought that, if she allowed it, he would have joined her in the shower, such was his need to stay as close as possible.

Wrapped in a towel, she walked back to her bedroom, stopping to firmly close the door to the sitting room. She couldn't bear the sight of the empty mirror.

With no thought to how she looked, which she would have known was terrible had she looked into the mirror, Ashlynne yanked on a pair of jeans, a tank top, and her tennis shoes and wound her still-wet hair up into a messy bun by feel to avoid the mirror. She left her room in search of coffee and to feed Murphy.

At the top of the stairs, curiosity got the better of her and she turned around to peek into Stella's room. It was immaculately clean and completely devoid of any personal items. She tiptoed in and carefully opened the closet door—nothing, just empty hangers on the rods.

Extra curious now, Ashlynne opened drawers and checked the bathroom. There was no indication that anyone had ever been there. Crossing the bathroom to Camryn's adjoining room, she found the same lack of personal items. The same situation was the case across the landing in the room that Riley had occupied.

Ashlynne ran up to the third floor and found more of the same, all drawers and closets were empty, all sheets clean, and beds made up to perfection. Even Bennette was gone.

"Where has everyone gone, Meredith?" Ashlynne asked quietly as she poured a cup of coffee.

"Everyone?" asked Meredith feigning ignorance.

"Yes. Everyone. As in everyone who trapped you in a doll and tried to kill me. Those people, Meredith," said Ashlynne in annoyance.

"I'm afraid I'm not sure what you're talking about, Ashlynne," answered Meredith very carefully.

Ashlynne gaped at her, "What do you mean you don't know what I'm talking about? Stella and Riley and the others of the coven, they're gone? And Bennette! Who was Bennette anyway?"

"Our guests have left for the season, Ashlynne, albeit early it would seem. The housekeepers have worked their magic, so to speak, and Rosehaven is now back to just being my home," said Meredith with a sly grin, "I am glad that you liked my friend Bennette. He's a man of few words but a very good soul, I think."

Ashlynne stood staring into her coffee, unsure how to proceed. She recognized the 'you've only been dreaming, Dorothy' ruse, but she strongly suspected that she wasn't going to get anything else out of Meredith, and honestly, she was a little afraid to try the Witch's patience.

"Um—OK, well…"

"Given that the guests have departed early, you are free to leave for home as soon as you would like. Of course, you are welcome to stay and enjoy the last of the summer if you would prefer. It's entirely up to you," interrupted Meredith as Ashlynne stumbled over her question. She added, "You will be paid for your original contract no matter your decision."

Ashlynne watched her leave for the gardens and looked at Murphy.

"What do you think, boy? Are you ready to go home?"

Murphy sat in his prettiest pose, ready for his breakfast and to go home to New Orleans.

Chapter 30

Ashlynne wasn't sure what she expected from her last day at Rosehaven, but the utter lack of goodbye from Meredith was a bit of a letdown. Of course, Eliza was gone so there was no farewell flicker of the lights, and the spirit of the Native American man was nowhere to be seen.

She rinsed her coffee cup out for the last time, filled her backpack with snacks for her and Murphy, and looked around the amazing kitchen with its sunroom and massive butcher-block table; she would miss it. Rosehaven was an enchanting and enchanted place even given the frightening and heartbreaking events that had occurred within its walls. No matter what, Ashlynne was positive that she would never find another house like it.

"Goodbye," she whispered.

Even though Eliza was gone, and Meredith was free, Rosehaven remained alive and aware—a true grande dame, if ever there was one, Ashlynne was certain.

Pulling the telescoping handle out from her rolling suitcase and clipping Murphy's leash to his harness, she dropped her key onto the scrap of paper that she had used to scribble a quick thank you note to Meredith. She walked through the butler's pantry to the service door one last time.

The house didn't seem nearly as imposing as it had when she first arrived, but then again, so much had changed in the past few weeks—herself included.

"Well, we did it, Murphy. We made it out alive. I have to admit, it was touch and go there for a little while," she said to the small dog who trotted cheerfully at her side.

The sun shone brightly through the mature hardwoods on Michigan Avenue, with the deeper glow of late summer rather than the brittle light of early May when she had arrived.

She crossed the bridge, stopping to take one more photograph of the red lighthouse, and watched as a pontoon boat full of kids and adults motored down the channel headed to Lake Michigan to spend a day on the water.

"It sure is a pretty little town, isn't it?" she asked the spirit in the cutaway waistcoat and top hat who stood next to them watching the sun sparkle on the water.

He smiled, tipped his hat, and walked back along the sidewalk where he melted into the crowd of living people who were waiting for a table on the balcony of the Weathervane where they would enjoy mimosas, chicken salad studded with dried cherries, and smoked whitefish dip with freshly baked bread. Summer in Charlevoix meant lunches like that as well as fireworks, festivals, art shows, beach stones, Witches, enchanted dolls, and the occasional ghost or two.

Ashlynne and Murphy boarded the small bus parked in the lot that shared space with the ferry that ran to and from Beaver Island. The bus was almost empty; hardly anyone was traveling south in the latter part of July as evidenced by the throngs of tourists boarding the ferry emblazoned with a bright green shamrock that would take them across the lake to the tiny island that shared a sister city in Ireland.

Ashlynne settled them both in a seat and sent a quick text to Andrew: *I'm coming home.*

As the bus pulled out of the parking lot and turned left onto Bridge Street, Ashlynne and Murphy watched the pretty shops and baskets of colorful petunias slide past as they rolled out of Charlevoix, headed south and to New Orleans.

Ashlynne pulled her sweater from her backpack, sent a silent prayer to Mimi, and closed her eyes to dream of Mardi Gras beads, street musicians, purple skies, and the broken and bumpy sidewalks of the French Quarter.

~The End~
February 26th, 2021
East Jordan, MI

Epilogue

Meredith heard the click-clack of the dog's nails on the hardwood floors below and the service door close with a thunk, signaling the final exit of Ashlynne and Murphy from Rosehaven. With a sigh born of both exhaustion and satisfaction, Meredith stepped from her suite onto the second-floor landing and pulled the door shut behind her. Using the tip of her finger she traced the sigil on the wood that would keep her space secure from any who chose to enter—be it physically or in spirit form.

"Do you think that is still necessary?"

The serene voice of Bennette made her start. Composing herself before turning and addressing him she replied, "I prefer maintenance magic over band-aid magic, you know that."

"Yes, I suppose so. Your training has so far stood you well. Training and a good amount of luck."

"There is no such thing as luck, Bennette. I am prepared for even the most outlandish attempts at unseating me," she answered.

Meredith moved past the Monk and started down the main staircase. The sun shone through the tall second-floor landing windows and hit the crystals that dangled from the massive chandelier resulting in a rainbow speckled aura that danced around her honey blonde hair. Bennette noticed the light-play with wry amusement; the suggestion of a halo was hard to miss, and he wondered if the Witch had produced the effect on purpose.

As he crossed the landing to follow Meredith down the stairs, Bennette couldn't help but note the closed door at the opposite end of the space from Meredith's own suite of rooms and recall the events that had occurred within.

His heart was heavy with the loss of an old friend, but Mimi had known that her time within the In Between was limited and that it had an ultimate goal. Even so, Bennette ached knowing what a sacrifice she had made for one so dear to her.

Meredith stepped from the main staircase and onto the plush wool rug that covered the hardwood floor of the main foyer.

The music room opened directly in front of her and, taking a moment to gaze at the empty table where she had stood, imprisoned within the doll for so many weeks, she purposely shut out the internal musings of the Monk who followed her downstairs. His emotional attachments to both the spirit, Mimi, and the young woman, Ashlynne, left her feeling tired and burdened. She had learned a long time ago to not allow such entanglements; it made a tricky life much trickier.

"Meredith, we need to talk about what happened here," he prompted.

"I suppose so," she replied over her shoulder to Bennette who had come to stand behind her. A hard smile etched itself on her otherwise pretty features and, while the Monk couldn't see the Witch's face, he could hear all he needed to know in the reply. Despite all that had happened he felt a twinge of pity for the members of the Dark Grove Coven.

Meredith turned left and entered the formal dining room, Bennette in her wake. While she was intensely private and would have preferred to keep this last bit of information to herself, she knew that manners required her to provide Bennette a finale. He had, after all, provided invaluable assistance to her.

Reaching into the pocket of her blouse for the heavy skeleton key that would open the various cabinets and curios in the dining room, Meredith stepped in front of the largest cabinet made up of drawers at the base and a top section of glass-fronted display shelves.

Bennette moved to her side and watched as she inserted the antique key into the ornate brass keyhole, unlocking it and swinging the doors open.

He peered inside. There were four shelves within the open cabinet, each holding line after line of ornate, delicately hued figurines. From a Goose-girl to a boy with a dog, to a romantic Mermaid, and Lovers embracing on a park bench each of the figurines showed the incredible detail that Italian porcelain is known for, and each stared out at him with curiously human eyes. All in all, there were over a dozen of them.

"I see," Bennette said to the Meredith, his voice clipped and hard as he turned away from the cabinet and the terrified eyes of Riley, now trapped in a figurine of a lady holding a parasol.

"Where do you think they learned their little trick, Bennette?" she replied, matching his tone.

Bennette tore his eyes away from the shelves of trophies and turned to face Meredith who held a dark green stone with a shimmering white band of quartz running unbroken around its length.

378

Preview for:
The Mirror Dance: A French Quarter Faerie Tale
The Faerie Tale Chronicles - Book 3

The young girl ran up the narrow dirt path as the sun sent its first weak rays over the horizon. The tall grasses lining either side of the path hung heavy with early morning dew that left her shoes and stockings sodden and heavy. Tomorrow would be La'Bealtaine and there was much to get ready before then. She pushed on, despite the discomfort of wet feet and legs, looking forward to warming her cold toes by the hearth in the manor's kitchen.

Turning the sharp bend that signaled the end of the meadow's path and the beginning of the manicured grounds of the manor, the smells and sounds of the great house drifted over her, carried on the early morning breezes; fresh bread baking in the rounded stone ovens and the sharp tang of early Gairleog Mhuire, or Crow Garlic, gathered to flavor soups and other savories for the festival. The lowing of cows ready to be milked and the sharper tones of the geese as they made their rounds about the packed dirt of the courtyard. The cook's guttural rebuke of a small child and the slapping sound as one large meaty hand met one bony buttock caused her to pick up her pace. The girl had been on the receiving end of that hand more times than she cared to remember and wanted not at all to add another incident to the list.

The cantankerous flock of geese scattered noisily as she ran past ensuring that no secretive entrance would be available to her, and she hoped that she wasn't too late. As she rounded the corner and slid into the kitchen the recent recipient of the cook's ire skirted past her, tears making clear tracks in the otherwise dirt-caked skin along his cheeks.

"' Tis time ye made it," came the gruff voice of the woman bent over a large kettle of pottage, her ample behind obscuring most of the hearth.

"The Lady would have ye attend her. Wipe yer face and put on a clean apron then be about it-I'll not be in trouble for yer laziness."

Mary kept her eyes down as she slipped on a clean apron and used her soiled one to wipe her shoes and stockings, only managing to smear the path's mud more evenly rather than wipe it clean away. Being summoned by the Mistress of the house was neither an honor nor a privilege and she could feel her heart beating against her ribs like a trapped and terrified bird. She stood up and seeing that there would be no more words of comfort- or otherwise -from the cook who was more inclined to cover her ample behind than protect the younger workers in her charge, Mary left the warmth of the kitchen and crossed the courtyard to the main house.

As a day worker, Mary was not afforded the luxury of servant status and was therefore not provided a room or a cot. She was paid in seasonal produce and a small amount of meat that she brought back to her family's cottage which added much-needed sustenance to their meager holdings. Her father and brothers worked the fields and pastures of the manor house in exchange for the rent of the land on which their home sat, while her mother and younger sisters tended to the small kitchen garden and livestock. Their dairy cow was allowed to graze on the manor's ridge with the other tenant's cows and was driven back every evening by the young boy who lived a field over to the west- his cajoling and cursing signaled the end of the small group of cottages workdays as regular as the seasons. Mary was sent to the Big House as a day worker in the hopes of being hired on as a servant, a position seen as a step up and out of the cottage. With exposure to the practices and patterns of the higher classes, Maggie O'Neil hoped for a better life for her eldest daughter. That the owners of the Big House were middling, at best, on the country's social ladder meant nothing to the thoughtful and ambitious woman on the bottom-most rung; a rung or two up was better than the bottom as far as she was concerned.

The haughty housekeeper stood at the entry, holding the heavy wooden door open to the dim interior of the hall. Following the imposing figure, Mary walked quickly over the uneven fieldstone trying not to slip on the unfamiliar flooring, being used to as she was of pounded earth strewn with rushes and grasses. Her toes caught on jutting edges of the roughly fitted stone and her footfalls echoed from the floors, bouncing off limed walls and stone moldings. For all the manor house's artistic improvements over her family's one-room cottage, Mary found it nonetheless cold and inhospitable.

The housekeeper stepped aside and pushed the skinny dark-haired girl through a heavy tapestry that hung from the beams of the ceiling, sectioning one space within the large room from another. As the curtain fell closed the housekeeper made a quick sign of the cross, a ritual that would brand her a Papist in this Protestant household and spell her immediate banishment, if not imprisonment, if it were seen by her employers.

As Mary's eyes adjusted to the sudden gloom she heard the sound of hooves on stone and wondered why the Big House would have animals within, a practice common to the poorer cottages but unheard of in the higher classes.

"My Lady?" whispered Mary into the gloom, trying desperately to make out the type of animal that was in the alcove with them. There was no scent of cow or sheep, only the sharp tang of medicinal herbs and plants that made up her mistress's toilet.

"Mary O'Neil. Thank you for attending me," came her mistress's Scottish brogue from deep within the shadows. The clip-clop of hooves on the stone had ceased.

"Of course, my Lady," whispered Mary, dropping a courtesy despite the lack of light. If her Mistress would see her and noted the lack of respect a thrashing would certainly follow. Though, given the Lady's known volatile temperament, a thrashing or tongue lashing could happen anyway. Aisla Drummond was well known in the region for her unpredictable nature and her Scottish Highlander roots, one contributing to the other in equal measure as far as the local Irish peasantry was concerned.

A candle flared as flame was set to wick and Aisla's burnished copper hair framing her ivory skin emerged from the shadows. Mary had never seen her Mistress, but her visage had been described in detail from cottage to cottage with lurid stories detailing how her skin stayed line free and smooth. Mary had little use for stories and assumed that the woman's perfect skin was a lucky happenstance of not having to work the fields or be subjected to the harsh summer sun's rays.

Dipping another curtsy to be on the safe side and keeping her eyes positioned down yet not so far down as to not be able to peak at the woman who summoned her, Mary waited for her instructions. Her heart still tripped painfully within her chest, and she would be very glad to be done here and attend to her kitchen duties where the dangers were known and easily avoided.

"Please come in, I've set tea," purred Aisla as she lit two more candles from the first and set them on the ledges that surrounded the small space.

Mary bobbed her head and moved further into the room expecting that she was being tested in the laying of the tea accouterments for further work in the Big House. How proud her mother would be! Lifting her head to better see what was being asked of her, Mary stopped in surprise. The scrubbed wooden table was already set with cups, saucers, a tea pot, and a small jar of honey. Biscuits were laid out on a small platter with cream and jam to the side of that. It was lovely and smelled wonderful. Most importantly it was done and therefore Mary had no idea what was expected of her.

"My Lady?" she said to the woman who sat watching her, a sly smile playing on her lips.

"Please sit Mary," she said as she walked around the small table and pulled a chair out for the dumbstruck girl.

Because doing as she was told was second nature to her, Mary walked to the proffered chair and sat down. She felt like she might be sick, surely this was not right. A thin white arm reached over her shoulder and poured the fragrant tea into the small cup and added a drop of honey to it. Next, a biscuit with jam was placed on the small plate in front of her. Aisla's voice purred from behind her, "The jam is from our own hedgerow's berries and is so very delicious, please try some."

Again, despite her growing fear, Mary did as she was told and took a bite of the biscuit. At any other time, it might have been delightful but for the terrified child stuck in this unpredictable tea party its sweetness was cloying and the cookie dry as dust. She sipped at her tea to help swallow the crumbs stuck in her throat when a sharp burning along her neck caused her to start and spill the hot liquid onto her clean apron.

"Ssshhhh, my dear. Sshhhh," whispered the redhead as she took the delicate teacup from Mary's hand and wrapped one bare white arm around the girl's thin shoulders. Using her other hand, Aisla pushed Mary's head to the side, her right ear almost touching her right shoulder to expose her neck. The pain grew stronger as Mary's skin was pulled taught. Frozen like a hare in fear and confusion, she could only stare wide-eyed at the flickering candles lined up along the wall as the Lady of the House continued to gouge deep wounds along her neck, bending to lap the beaded blood like a contented house cat with a saucer of cream.

The candles had long since burned down when Mary O'Neil awoke in the darkened chamber; cold, confused, and sore. Lines of fiery pain shot down her neck from her hairline to her collarbone. Disjointed memories of a pale-faced redhead who served her tea and biscuits and the clip-clop of hooves on stone looped over and over in her head remaining fuzzy and unclear no matter how hard she tried to recall the assault.

Still shaky, Mary stood carefully and gripped the edge of the table for balance. Despite her watery memory of a tea party of sorts, the table was empty save for a lone candle burned to a nub in its holder.

As she made her way back into the main room and out into the courtyard Mary was stunned to see that the sun had set and darkness had begun to pool from the corners and edges of the manor house, the kitchen, and the stables spilling out into the courtyard like molasses. She made her way across the yard and entered the kitchen where the cook was kneading balls of bread dough; her sleeves pushed up past her elbows, arms the size of hams, dusted in flour.

"Ma'am, I—," whispered Mary.

"Yer supper is on the hearth, though I doubt it will be fresh now. Eat it up, you need your strength. Then wash your bowl and go home, it's late and I don't want your Mam yellin' at me that you're out past dark," interrupted the large woman. The tone was abrupt, devoid of concern, and yet somehow knowing.

"What happened?" asked Mary in a small voice.

"Nothing has happened. Nothing. You fell asleep and the Mistress was kind enough to let you nap. Eat and go home, now- 'tis late.

Mary took her bowl from the hearth and removed the linen that had been placed over it. A pottage of potatoes and peas with a couple of onion slices for flavoring had congealed within the wooden container. Seeing that the cook was watching to see that she ate, she spooned the mass of mushy vegetables and starches into her mouth and swallowed quickly, praying that it would stay down. While she still felt shaky and weak, her stomach was rebelling at the addition of the food. All she wanted was her own bed and her own family.

Taking a dipper of water from next to the

breadboard, she wiped her mouth and turned to go.

"Leave the apron, it's the House's," barked the cook. Mary slipped the closest thing to a uniform that she had over her head and dropped it next to the table.

Watching the skinny child shuffle down the trail away from the manor, the Cook took the apron -still stained with blood - and tossed it onto the fire, watching as the flames consumed the only evidence of what had happened to the girl.

"Will this one take?" the older woman asked the cat that sat next to the window. "Tomorrow is the great festival and if this one doesn't work, we will be burnin' aprons for the next year."